Aberdeenshire
COUNCIL
Aberdeenshire Libraries
www.aberdeenshire.gov.uk/libraries
Renewals Hotline 01224 661511
HQ
D1334776

Books

Secrets & Spies

Treason

Plague

Inferno

New World

Jo Macauley

Secrets & Spies

Inferno

First published in 2013 by Curious Fox,
an imprint of Capstone Global Library Limited,
7 Pilgrim Street, London, EC4V 6LB
Registered company number: 6695582

www.curious-fox.com

Series created by Hothouse Fiction
www.hothousefiction.com

Cover design by samcombes.co.uk

ISBN 978 1 78202 042 4

1 3 5 7 9 10 8 6 4 2

A CIP catalogue for this book is available from the British Library.

Typeset in Adobe Garamond Pro by Hothouse Fiction Ltd

Printed and bound by CPI Group (UK) Ltd, Croydon, CRO 4YY

With special thanks to Martyn Beardsley

Prologue

London, August 1666

Oranges and lemons, say the bells of Saint Clement's.

You owe me five farthings, say the bells of Saint Martin's.

When will you pay me, say the bells of Old Bailey...

"Sing it with me, Lucinda – it's the bit about when I grow rich next!"

The little girl sat on the doorstep of her small, ramshackle house in Bloodbone Alley, Shadwell, merrily singing her favourite song and bouncing her rag doll by its arms. It was late summer and the sun was hanging in a clear blue sky above the roof of the inn across the road. The brown Thames rolled by at the end of the

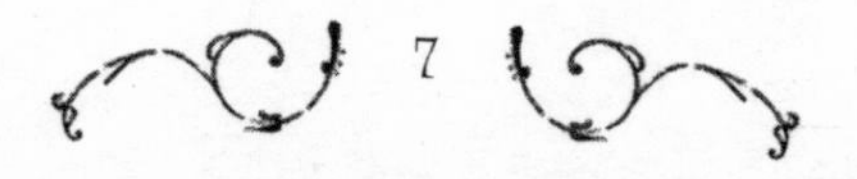

alley, and the girl could see a small merchant ship and a couple of coal barges at anchor at the landing stage. A small group of children who lived in this East London alley were playing a boisterous ball game close by, but the girl with the doll couldn't join in the fun. Her thin, almost useless legs were spread out on the dusty ground before her, and a pair of walking sticks leaned against the wall. But she didn't mind. She had been like this since before she could remember, and it was the only way of life she had known. She enjoyed just being around the other children and losing herself in her own colourful little world.

But before she could launch into the next verse of her song, there was a cry of "*Catch*!" and the tallest of the boys in the little gang playing nearby sent a gentle toss her way. The girl smiled. They knew she couldn't join properly, but they always tried to include her in whatever way they could. She managed to catch the ball and threw it back to the boy, who gave her a cheery wave then went back to the game with the other children.

"That was a good throw, wasn't it Lucinda? Straight into his hands from all this way away. If only our legs worked properly, we would show them how good we'd be at their games!"

She assumed that no one but Lucinda, with her yellow hair, permanent cheery smile and cheeks painted rosy-red, had heard her.

But she was wrong.

With the sun behind the inn across the road, its doorway was cast deep in shadow – and hidden within that darkness was a short but stocky man, watching the children at play.

The inn was called The Pelican, but the locals knew it as the Devil's Tavern after the smugglers and other unsavoury characters that frequented it at night.

Soon, a younger boy with red hair threw the ball towards the seated girl once more, but in his excitement his throw was too hard, too wide. It hit the wall beside her and bounced across the alley. Just as the boy was about to retrieve it, the figure in the doorway of the Pelican emerged, picked it up, and tossed it back.

"Uh … thanks," the red-haired boy said in an uncertain tone. There was something about the man that unnerved him – not least the missing finger on the hand that had tossed the ball.

The man didn't say a word in reply, and returned to the shadows.

As evening drew in, a couple of the children were

called in by their mothers. Their ball game was winding down, and the remaining three children stood in a circle, chatting and half-heartedly throwing the ball between each other – but it was suppertime now, and soon they waved to the girl and said their goodbyes. The red-haired boy was one of them. He cast a wary glance in the direction of The Pelican's doorway.

"How will you get indoors? Do you need a hand?" he called to the crippled girl.

"Oh, I'll be all right," she said, jabbing her thumb towards her sticks. "Anyway, I'm waiting for my brother to come home from work. He always gives me a big hug and carries me indoors!"

"Well, don't stay out too late, or the bogeyman will get you!" laughed a girl as they departed.

The red-haired boy frowned and looked towards the door once more. "Don't say things like that," he chided.

"Oh, we don't believe in the bogeyman, do we Lucinda?" the seated girl said to her doll.

But as soon as the coast was clear, the bogeyman, or at least the closest thing to one she would ever encounter, was already creeping from his hiding place. The girl had her back to him. His stealthy footsteps brought him closer by the second. She heard a movement behind her

at the last moment, but it was already too late. She was scooped up from the ground in a pair of brawny arms and carried quickly towards a coach that was waiting round the corner. As her captor hurried along the street, he placed a great paw of a hand over her mouth to prevent her screams being heard by the inhabitants of Shadwell. But although the girl's withered legs dangling helplessly, she wriggled her body and thrashed with her arms for all she was worth. A man emerged from the coach to help the kidnapper get her inside, and in the struggle a handkerchief fell from his pocket. Once their victim was safely inside, the two men joined her. The driver cracked his whip, and the wheels of the carriage clattered as the coach disappeared in a cloud of dust.

Chapter One

Flavia

There was an excited buzz running through the cast standing on the stage of the otherwise empty King's Theatre. All the actors gathered in little huddles chattering animatedly, awaiting the announcement the theatre manager William Huntingdon was about to make. All, that was, except Beth Johnson.

"And our next production," Huntingdon declared, "will be the acclaimed *dramatic* production – *The Empire Dies*!"

A ripple of excitement went through the group, but Beth's heart sank. She stood slightly apart from the rest,

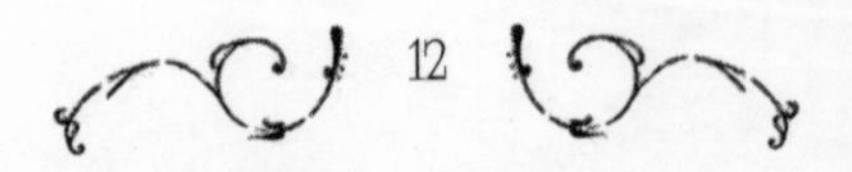

chewing her lip. With her tall, willowy figure, long, chestnut-brown hair and pretty green eyes, she was used to being the King's Players' leading lady. In the few short years she'd been with them, she had established herself as the most popular actress in London. But her parts had all been in light-hearted productions or out-and-out comedies. This was different. Would she be offered *any* role, let alone the lead? Did Huntingdon believe she was capable of serious acting? Beth wasn't even sure herself...

"And *The Empire Dies* will be different in other ways too," Huntingdon continued, as he sat in the front row of the auditorium with his assistant beside him. He had been a fine actor himself in his day, and his powerful voice echoed around the majestic theatre and its three tiers of empty seating. "This production calls for big set-piece scenes with lots of extras. We need to make it a big success, because it will cost more to produce than our last three plays put together. As well as all the additional actors and actresses, I shall be having a trap door cut into the stage, a flying machine is to be installed and we shall be employing fireworks at various points during the performance!"

At this, more excited chatter moved through the gathered players.

"But the parts, the parts!" cried Benjamin Lovett, Beth's only adversary among the cast. "Who shall play Constantine? Who, Alaric, leader of the Goths? I should just like to mention that I have studied Alaric in the history books – his speeches, his mannerisms, the gallant way he—"

"Please, Mister Lovett," interjected Huntingdon. "I have, of course, given the matter a lot of thought. Some of you who have not had the chance to blossom in comedy may prove to be dramatic actors of power and depth. Equally, those of you who are rightly lauded for your comedic performances may find this tragedy not to your suiting…"

Beth groaned inwardly. He wasn't looking directly at her, yet she felt sure he was preparing her for the bad news. She imagined herself being issued with the costume of a Roman peasant girl…

"Benjamin," Huntingdon said. "You are to play an important role – that of Alaric's opponent, the Emperor Honorius!"

"B-but he *loses*!" Lovett wailed.

"Uh, yes, Rome does eventually fall – but what a magnificent defeat! What a wonderfully tragic hero! I believe, Benjamin, that only *you* can achieve the

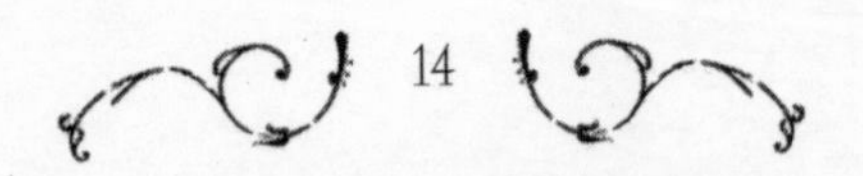

right balance between heroism and noble defeat in the same character."

"Plus," old Matthew the prompter chipped in from the wings, "no one else wanted the part!"

Laughter echoed around the theatre, but it was quickly silenced by a stern glare from Huntingdon. "That is certainly not true. So, Benjamin, what say you?"

Lovett hesitated, and Beth could almost see into his mind as he mentally rehearsed the triumphant smiles, the tragic grimaces and gestures that would surely feature prominently in his interpretation of the role.

"Very well – I accept!"

There were sighs of relief all round. Then Huntingdon turned his gaze on Beth, and her heart skipped a beat. She steeled herself for the disappointment, the embarrassment of losing her place as the company's lead actress. She could even hear his words before he uttered them: *Beth, you are a fine comedy actress, but...*

"Beth, my dear," began the theatre manager, "you are a fine comedy actress, but I am equally sure that you can bring depth and feeling to a serious role – and thus you are our Flavia. She is the leading lady, the Roman noblewoman who falls for Alaric and is torn between betraying her people and supporting her lover."

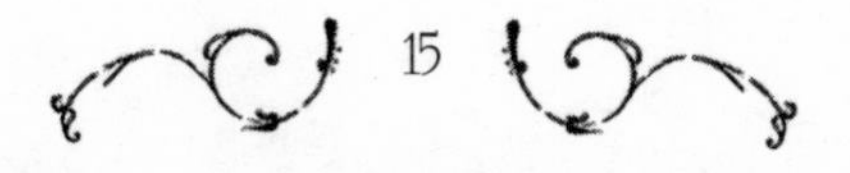

There was spontaneous applause, and Beth felt slaps of congratulations on her back, but she herself hadn't quite taken it in. The main female role in a major dramatic play? But Benjamin Lovett's reaction was very predictable.

"*That* part must be played by a mature woman, not a little girl who only knows how to slap her thigh and make merry," he muttered.

"Don't listen to him, Mistress Beth!"

She felt herself being squeezed tightly by Maisie White. The young orange-seller had been standing a little to the side of the auditorium, but rushed up to hug her friend Beth on hearing the news. The two of them had been like sisters since Beth had found the younger girl begging in Covent Garden. She discovered that after Maisie's mother had died, she had stowed away in a ship from America to come in search of her father. The echoes of her own life – she herself had been abandoned as a child – had drawn her immediately to the pretty orphan with the dark curls and bright blue eyes.

"He has got a point," Beth said tentatively. "I've never played a big, serious role in my life. How do I know I can even do it? I *am* only a young woman and Flavia was much older. Will audiences believe in me?"

"*I* believe in you, Beth. And it could have been worse."

"What do you mean?"

"If Mister Huntingdon had given you the part of Messalina you would probably have had to be in *love* scenes with Benjamin Lovett!"

They both looked at each other for a moment, then cried "Yuck!" in unison.

"MAISIE WHITE!"

Huntingdon's voice boomed out from the front seats of the theatre.

The girl instantly fell silent, her face glowing red. "Sorry, Mister Huntingdon sir, I was just..."

"I don't want you selling oranges in this theatre when we stage *The Empire Dies*, Maisie."

Beth frowned indignantly, unsure whether to intervene. She could see that poor Maisie was on the verge of tears.

"But, sir! I only wanted to congratulate Beth. I know I'm not supposed to come on to the stage but—"

"Well you had better get *used* to being on stage. I need lots of extras for this play and you are to be one of them. A high-ranking Roman lady, the wife of a member of the Senate."

Maisie gawped at Huntingdon as if he had grown

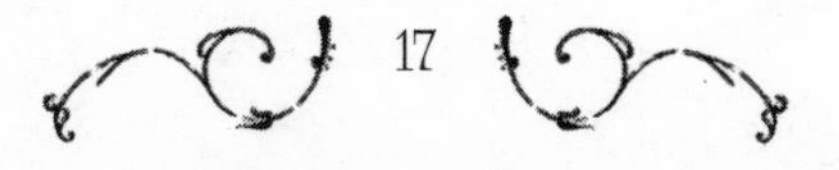

another head. "But I … you can't possibly … me?"

"What are you standing there for, child? Go and get measured up for a costume!"

Now it was Beth's turn to hug Maisie. She knew that the only thing that meant more to her friend than finding her father was her dream of treading the boards herself. This was a small start – but it was a start.

Huntingdon went through the rest of the cast list, then picked up a pile of scripts from the seat next to his and made his way to the stage. "I want the principal players to gather round for the first read-through."

The cast formed a circle around Huntingdon, who moved to sit in an old wooden chair in the centre of the stage. Beth sat cross-legged next to Samuel Jones, the actor chosen to play Alaric, the lead male part. He was quite a bit older than her but very handsome and a favourite with all the girls at the King's Theatre.

Beth began to read her lines, but was soon interrupted.

"I can't hear her!" Benjamin Lovett complained. He was sitting at the edge of the circle on a chair because his podgy legs wouldn't allow him to sit cross-legged on the floor. Huntingdon ignored him.

"Let us move to Scene Four – Flavia's chamber at midnight," he announced instead. He didn't look in

Lovett's direction, but in a quieter voice he addressed Beth directly. "And try to project a little more please, Flavia."

Beth cleared her throat nervously. If she wasn't even good enough to play a serious part, how could she even think of ever fulfilling her own dream of running a theatre company?

By the end of the cast's very first run through the script, they all smiled warmly and congratulated her before they parted. But as the rest of cast began to disperse, Huntingdon discreetly took Beth to one side, and she feared the worst.

"Can we have a brief word, please?"

"You don't think I can do it, do you—?" Beth began

"Are you accusing me of having poor judgement?" he asked her sternly, but with a twinkle in his eye.

"Oh no, Mister Huntingdon. But I *know* others couldn't hear me as well as Mister Lovett and, well…"

"Projecting the voice doesn't come naturally, Beth. 'Tis a skill we've all had to learn. The comedies you have been used to tend to be fast, furious and loud anyway, but tragedies have many more serious and quiet moments. The trick is, how to be quiet yet still ensure you can be heard by all."

"But what does that mean?"

Huntingdon arranged two chairs opposite each other on the now otherwise empty stage, and they both sat.

"First, think about the way you breathe…"

Beth's intensive lesson on projection lasted a good forty-five minutes. Huntington taught her about posture, breathing, relaxing the throat and bringing the sound forward. By the time she and Maisie were on their way home, she was feeling much better about tackling the dream role she had been given.

"What was Mister Huntingdon talking to you about for so long?" Maisie asked, as they walked along Drury Lane towards the Peacock and Pie tavern where they lived. Autumn was almost upon them, but Beth felt as hot and sweaty as she had all through this long, dry summer. She wiped beads of sweat from her brow.

"He was teaching me a special way to talk."

"But you can already talk…"

"Yes! But inside a theatre, the normal way of talking doesn't always work."

"So, have you got to learn to talk in French or something, then?"

Beth laughed. "No! It's to do with making sure everyone can hear you."

"There's so much to learn. My Roman lady's costume is beautiful, I just won't know what to *do* in it!"

"Well, you won't have to say any lines in your first stage role. Don't worry, I'll help you with everything."

Big Moll, the landlady of the Peacock and Pie, greeted the girls warmly the instant they crossed the threshold of the tavern. She was carrying a big rolled-up carpet under one brawny arm, as easily as if it were a piece of parchment. "Well, here comes me little beauties!" she said. "Maisie, can you fetch some water for me from the well in the garden? Mind you don't fall down, though. The water's got so low the bucket's scraping the bottom. We need a bit o' rain, that's what we need."

"Yes, Moll," said Maisie.

"Good girl. As soon as I've beaten the dust out of this I'll prepare you both a nice bit o' supper."

"Thank you," said Beth. "We'll be in the little side room if you don't mind. Maisie's going to be in the next play and I'm going to help her with a few things."

"I'm to be an important Roman lady!" Maisie declared, her blue eyes beaming like sapphires.

"Well I never," said Moll, chuckling.

As soon as Maisie had fetched the water, they went into the room off the main drinking area that was

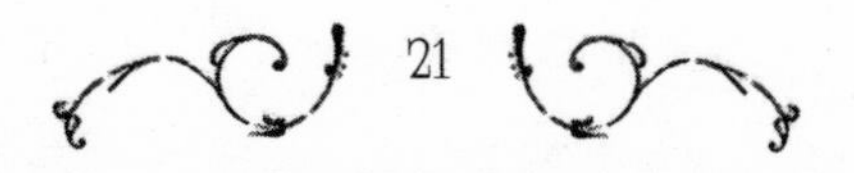

sometimes let out to gentlemen who required a little privacy, and Beth began their first lesson.

"Now, face the window and imagine it's where the audience is sitting..."

Maisie went pale. "Audience? Oh – they'll all be looking at me!"

"That's the general idea, Maisie! But anyway, they'll be looking at *everyone* all the time, depending on what's happening and who's speaking."

"Good ... although I do hope they look at me a little. My costume is so splendid, t'would be a shame if—"

But they were interrupted by a desperate hammering at the door to their little room.

"Come in!" said Beth, surprised.

The door flew open, and in came a rather dishevelled boy of about Beth's age.

"John!" she exclaimed.

Beth hadn't seen her friend – and fellow spy – John Turner for some weeks. Unbeknownst to all who knew her – including Maisie – as well as being a celebrated actress, Beth was also secretly working in the service of the King. She had been recruited by mysterious spymaster Sir Alan Strange, and had been leading a double life ever since. John, too, had become an undercover spy.

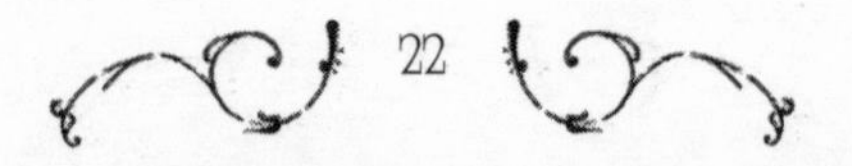

He'd shown great prowess, having become inadvertently involved in one of Beth's missions to stop an attempt on the King's life. She eyed him closely now, wondering if he had come bearing news of an assignment…

"What brings you here?" she said, glancing at Maisie warily.

It looked as if he'd run all the way from his home in Shadwell, and he paused for a moment to recover his breath. "Moll told me you'd be in here. I-I need to speak to you about an important matter…"

"Uh, just a moment." Beth turned to her young friend. "Maisie, we're upstage, facing downstage. Stage left is that side, and stage right is the other. I want you to pretend Mister Huntingdon is giving you instructions, and then walk from one area to the other. Remind yourself inwardly what part of the stage you are on. *And* I want you to walk with your back straight as if you are carrying a tray of pies without dropping them. Can you do that while I talk to John?"

"I'll certainly give it a try!"

"That's the spirit!" Beth took John into the room next door, which was thankfully empty. "Sit down, John," she said quietly. "What is it?"

"'Tis my sister Polly. She has disappeared a-and

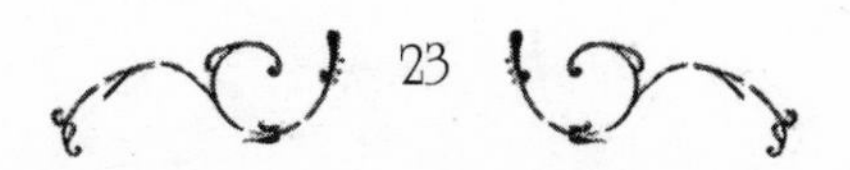

it's all my fault!"

"Take a deep breath," Beth said, holding up one hand. "What do you mean?"

"Well, she likes to sit outside watching the other children play, and I usually come to take her indoors after work…"

"And when you arrived today she was no longer there?"

"Yes! I was about to hurry home to tend to her, but I was obliged to remain at the Navy Board. There are big plans to build a new warship, the biggest in the navy yet. It is to be named after the King, and he is visiting our offices soon to see the plans, so we had to work late. When I finally got home, she was nowhere to be seen."

Beth swallowed. "My goodness. But you must not blame yourself, John, I'm sure she'll be found soon enough," she said, trying her best to sound encouraging.

"But that isn't all…"

"Oh?"

"I was talking to the children she was playing with, and one of them said he saw a stranger standing in the shadows of the inn across the alley, watching them play."

"But men can often be found outside inns. Waiting for a friend, or waiting for—"

"He was short and stocky – and he was missing a finger on his left hand," John said grimly.

Beth had been trying to play down John's fears for his sister, but now she couldn't hide her own shock at hearing this news. "*Groby?*"

Edmund Groby was a renowned anti-royalist thug, who'd been involved in more than one attempt on the King's life as the henchman of the criminal mastermind and conspirator Sir Henry Vale. He had a distinct gait and an ominously missing finger…

"I fear he's back to take revenge for my role in foiling his plots in the past. I fear he's going to kill my baby sister!" John was ashen, slumped in the chair.

Beth shook her head slowly as she sifted through what John had told her. "If it was simply revenge, with all the other children gone he could have easily killed her there and then, with no witnesses. There is more to this. He might be an evil man but everything he does is in the cause of a republic and against the King; as far as we know he is not a killer of little girls."

"Then why take her?"

"I'll wager he wants something in return for her safety."

John was not reassured. "If it's something we cannot

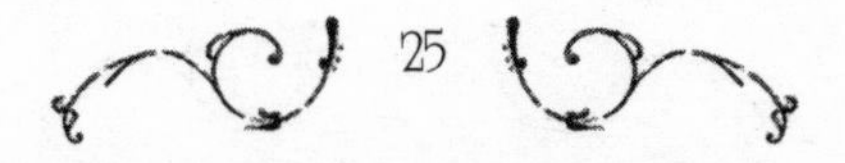

give him, he *will* kill her!"

Beth straightened her back. "The main thing is that Polly is almost certainly still alive. We have beaten Groby and his gang before, and we can do it again."

Chapter Two

Ransom

"Knowing Sir Alan Strange," said Beth, "he's probably already aware Groby's back in England."

Having made her excuses, she'd left the Peacock and Pie with John and they were on their way to the bookshop of a mysterious man named Joad on Ludgate Hill. They needed to report to their spymaster urgently – but meetings with him were only on his terms, and to arrange one at such short notice they first had to visit Joad. The shop was set back a little from the rest of the buildings, and seemed like a forgotten remnant of centuries past. It was crooked, leaning to one side as if about to fall against its neighbour, and with little windows like staring eyes defying anyone to come too close. Beth had never seen anyone enter the shop to buy a book, and something about the place had always made her feel strangely ill at ease.

Joad himself was a peculiar, surly little man with long, greasy hair. He never smiled or looked Beth in the eye. When they entered today he was writing something in a ledger, but as soon as they entered he dropped his quill and slammed the book shut. A cloud of dust momentarily obscured his face and he didn't greet them. Beth knew protocol meant they had to speak first, and it had to be in coded words.

"I'm looking for a play by Fitzangelo…"

Joad grunted to himself before replying. "I have no works by that author. But there is a seller near St Bride's who might be able to help. Be quick about it, though – he closes his shop at six."

With that, Joad opened up his ledger, dipped his quill in the ink, and resumed his writing. Both Beth and John knew what his words meant, and without even bothering to reply they left the shop.

"The Bridewell Burial Ground at 6 p.m.?" John murmured as they set off.

But before he had even finished getting his words out, the bells of nearby St Clement's began to strike the hour of six.

"Yes. And Strange will only wait a quarter of an hour there. If we don't arrive by the time St Bride's strikes again at quarter past, he will leave," said Beth, quickening her pace.

The burial ground was to the rear of the grim quadrangle of buildings comprising a workhouse for the poor and a House of Correction known as Bridewell. Beth and John first headed for the river Fleet that flowed through the city from the north into the Thames – at least it usually did. After the summer drought it was little more than a smelly ditch with swarms of midges buzzing over it. Beth covered her mouth and nose with her hand, and they hurriedly took a short cut down Dorset Street. The place where the paupers of the area were buried was enclosed by crumbling walls and accessed by a rusting iron gate. It creaked as if in warning when John pushed it open. The high red-brick walls kept most of the sunlight out. What little light did enter the burial ground sent long

fingers of shadow running off the rows of gravestones and the withered trees in the centre. Beth cast her eyes all around the area, scrutinizing stone and wooden grave markers: uncared for, names fading, many leaning at crazy angles. She saw no sign of Strange. She and John walked cautiously along the cracked, sun-baked path towards the trees.

"He's not here," said John. "This place give me the creeps – let's go back and wait at the gate."

"It must be almost quarter past six. He should be here – unless he's given up waiting and gone already."

There was a sudden commotion behind the nearest headstone. John sprang back and Beth grabbed his arm in alarm, until they both saw the pigeon they'd startled flapping indignantly into the branches of one of the trees.

Beth's heart was pounding, and they both laughed nervously at their reactions.

"We should go, see if there's more news," John said agitatedly after a couple of minutes.

"You can go home once you've told me the purpose of this urgent meeting," came a deep voice. Spymaster Sir Alan Strange stepped out from behind one of the trees, his craggy face looking almost as if it were part of the

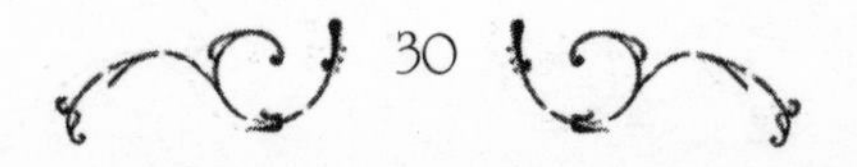

gnarled trunk itself.

"We think Groby is back in England," Beth began, wasting no time. To her surprise, Strange's expression didn't change and he merely nodded.

"I have had two other sightings in the past week from my sources – but he has proved elusive so far," he said.

"We think he's up to something," John added anxiously.

"Now that the worst of the plague is over, the King has returned to Whitehall. I have seen to it that there is extra protection for him – both seen, and unseen."

"But there's something else," John persisted. "M-my little sister ... has vanished, and I'm almost certain that a man fitting Groby's description was behind it."

Strange's features darkened as he considered this for a moment. "This is troubling ... But, John, until we are certain of what has occurred with your sister, we must assume nothing, and we must act with extreme caution where Groby is concerned. His re-emergence and your sister's disappearance may be unrelated. However difficult it may be for you, the protection of the King's life must always be your main goal, and we must to nothing to jeopardize that."

Beth could sense John's growing frustration. "Sir, it

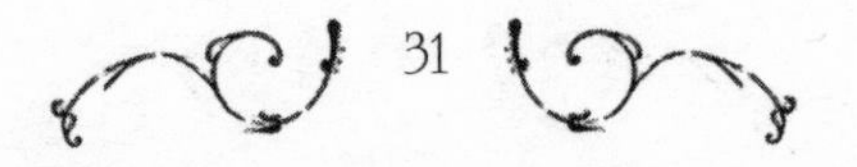

seems unlikely it could be anyone other than Groby. The child has only recently been taken. If we act quickly—"

Strange looked at them both sternly. "If her disappearance *is* related to another plot against His Majesty, then if you solve that, you will doubtless find the girl. Your assignment is clear. You must *not* alert the enemy to our investigations, but you must focus on finding out more about what Groby has planned. Protecting the King should be foremost in your priorities. I trust I have made myself clear."

With that, he strode briskly past them without a backwards glance, sending more pigeons flapping in panic for the tops of the walls. Beth and John watched in silence as he slipped through the gate and vanished into Dorset Street.

John shook his head. "It's as if Polly's life is of no importance to him," he said through clenched teeth.

Beth placed a hand on his arm, and held his gaze. "You must remember his mission is to keep the King safe. If plotters succeeded in killing the King, the whole country will be in turmoil once more. But he's probably right – the two things could be linked so stopping one would stop the other. And after all," she said reassuringly, "he didn't say we *couldn't* search for Polly."

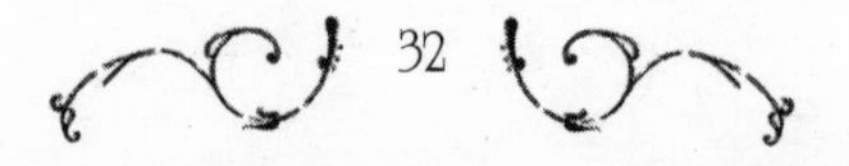

He said nothing, but smiling and looking at her gratefully, he reached over and squeezed her hand.

"I'll be with you all the way, John. I know you would do the same for me," Beth whispered.

"And more." He looked shyly at the ground for a moment before taking a deep breath. I need to get home to Shadwell and find out what news."

"I'll come with you," Beth said. "Let's go."

From the Tower Beth and John took the river path, where the cooler air beside the water made the atmosphere seem just a little fresher, despite the powerful stench of human and animal pollution. It was a couple of miles to Shadwell, past the wharves and warehouses along Thames Street. Men with barrels on carts were spraying water on the road in a vain attempt to stop the traffic throwing up the clouds of dust. Despite their efforts, it still drifted into houses and the eyes and noses of travellers.

When they got to Shadwell itself, John's friends, family and neighbours were roaming the streets knocking on doors and calling Polly's name. In spite of the heat, Beth pulled her light cloak hood over her head inconspicuously. Her growing popularity on the stage meant she was more easily recognized, and given the real, espionage-related association she and John had, she decided she'd rather not draw too much attention to herself. As they approached the Pelican Stairs at the water's edge a small boy came running towards them, and Beth hung back a little.

"We still can't find her anywhere!" he told John, alarm and anguish etched into his young features.

"Is Father out searching?" John asked quickly, and Beth realized this must be one of his brothers.

"He was, but he's at home comforting Mother now. She's mightily troubled..."

"Keep looking," John told the little boy, then glanced back at Beth and gestured for her to follow. He led them down Bloodbone Alley towards his family's little house, and Beth could hear a woman sobbing even before they got to the door. Beth waited just outside, knowing she shouldn't break cover to meet John's family, much though she wanted to offer them comfort. She listened closely.

"John! Any news? Has anyone found anything?"

"Sorry, Father. No news so far."

Beth heard Mr Turner sigh. "I'm afraid we have some, son."

"What do you mean?" John asked anxiously.

"This was pushed under our door," his father replied in a shaky voice. "It's a ransom note."

Chapter Three

Contact

"Give me the note, Father. Some of my contacts, uh, at the Navy Board … may be able to help with this. I'll be back."

John hurried outside, his face pale. Beth gave a low whistle to attract his attention to where she'd been waiting. Their eyes met worriedly, but they hurried away from the house a little before Beth reached out her hand for the note.

"This is good quality paper," she commented, turning it over in her hands.

"But the writing doesn't look like an educated hand. It's all in capitals."

"Probably to disguise the handwriting."

Beth turned her attentions to the message itself:

YOU NEED POLLY. WE NEED TO GET TO THE KING.
IF WE DONT GET WHAT WE NEED, YOU
WILL NEVER GET WHAT YOU NEED.
INSTRUCTIONS TO FOLLOW.

John swallowed hard. "This is what I feared. They mean to kill the King *and* my sister!"

"All is not lost, John. We have outwitted Groby before, and we can do it again. With Polly being so young, perhaps they won't restrain her as tightly as they would someone older. Perhaps … perhaps she will be able to slip through some open window and run until she finds—"

"No, Beth," John said sadly. "Polly can't run anywhere. She got the leg-wasting disease when she was three. She can only walk with the sticks that were found where she had been sitting in the street, and even with those she can't go very far or fast."

Beth sighed. "Well, surely Strange must listen to us now. This note is proof that Polly's kidnapping is clearly linked to a plot against the King. If he helps us track her,

the trail will also lead to us to the conspirators."

John brightened a little. "You're right."

"I doubt, though, whether we would be able to arrange to see Strange again tonight."

John looked out at the gathering darkness, and his face fell. "But there's no time to lose!"

Beth reached out a hand and rested it on John's shoulder. "I know it's difficult, but we'll have to wait until morning. You see what they've said in the note – there will be more of their instructions to follow. They won't harm Polly yet."

John nodded. "I had better get back."

Beth nodded, and gave his shoulder a squeeze. "I shall return at first light…"

It was a long and troubled night for John. He feared that in the urgency to find Groby his sister's whereabouts might be overlooked. What if he had passed her onto someone else? They might be seeking Groby out in one part of London with Polly somewhere else completely, her life hanging by a thread…

He drifted in and out of sleep, his mind like a

whirlpool of possibilities. At one point he heard the bellman's cry of "Past four of the clock and a warm, dry morning," but he must have dozed off again, because the next thing he knew he was aware of footsteps echoing in the empty alley below.

At first, he wasn't sure if it was just the product of his foggy, half-waking mind. But then he heard them again, coming to a shuffling halt below his window. He threw his bedcovers back and jumped out of bed, padding as quickly and quietly as he could down the stairs. As he hurried through the living room a flash of white at the foot of the door caught his eye, and he was just in time to see a letter being pushed under the gap. Ignoring it, he quickly undid the bolt and threw the door open, rushing out into the street.

Two men were striding away down Bloodbone Alley. Without a thought for his own safety, John raced up and grabbed one of them by the sleeve. The man spun round, yanking his arm free and lashing out with his other fist.

In the darkness, John never even saw the punch coming. He just felt an eye-watering crunch against his face, followed by the warm trickle of blood flowing from his nose, dripping from his chin and onto the cobbles as the men disappeared into the gloom of the morning.

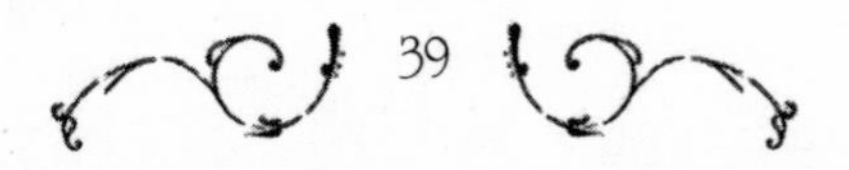

Chapter Four

Pirates' Dock

"*John!* What happened?" Beth exclaimed, seeing his reddened eye and the dark crusts of blood in his nostrils. She was shocked to see her friend's appearance when he answered her gentle knock at the door.

"I couldn't sleep … I heard someone outside and went to see, and got thumped for my troubles…"

"Are you all right?"

"I've had worse in fights at school."

"Was it Groby?" she said urgently.

He shook his head. "Unfortunately not. Though I'm sure I *would* be in a worse state if it had been."

Beth sighed and told him to go inside and bring a washcloth and basin. They moved a little distance away from the house, and sat down on some stone steps while she cleaned the dried blood from his face. As she worked, John reached into his pocket and produced a piece of paper that looked similar to one they'd received the previous day.

"They were delivering another message?"

He handed it to her and Beth put the cloth down to read it. There was a simple, child-like drawing of a doll at the top. Beneath that was writing in the same anonymous capital letters as the first message:

PROOF THAT WE HAVE HER.
BE AT PIRATES' DOCK AT EIGHT OF
THE CLOCK WITH A WAY TO REACH THE KING.
FAIL AND THE GIRL DIES.

"What does the picture of the doll mean?"

John stared at it, his eyes almost black with anger. "It's Lucinda."

"Lucinda?"

"Polly's doll. She would never be parted from it..." He clenched his jaw, and Beth gently reached over to

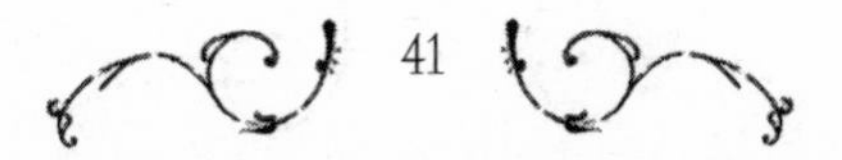

unfurl his hands, which were balled into fists. "I'll have to tell my family that they've demanded information about the Navy Board in return for Polly, and that I'm doing everything I can to get it. They can't know a plot against the King is involved."

"You're right. Still, we shall go along with their demands here," Beth told him firmly.

"But we can't betray the King!" John exclaimed.

"The King has a great deal of protection. Whatever they're planning can't happen straight away – they need the information. So it will give us time to figure out a plan. Polly is the one in the most immediate danger. We'll go to the meeting place and let's see what comes of it."

John swallowed. "Yes, that make sense. There's one problem, though…"

"What's that?"

"I don't know where Pirates' Dock is."

"Oh. Neither do I. But I thought with your work for the Navy Board…?"

"That's just it. There are lots of docks and places along the river I haven't been to, but I know the names of them all. I know for a fact that there is no Pirates' Dock – at least, not officially."

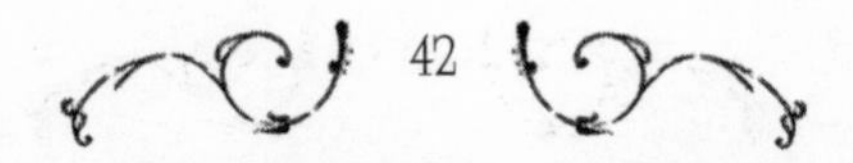

"Well, there would be no point in them trying to trick you," Beth said. "It *must* exist."

"And I know of only one person who knows the river better than me..."

Beth allowed herself a grin. "Ralph Chandler!"

It was still early morning when they left Bloodbone Alley, but by the time they reached Ralph's lodgings in Black Swan Alley there was bright sky above the fields beyond Whitechapel. Most of the houses and shops had not yet stirred, but in Walter Culpeper's shop they could see the tall figure of the herbalist mixing potions in flasks. John knocked hesitantly on the door, and the owner beckoned them in with a long, thin arm that emerged from the baggy sleeve of his black gown.

"We're sorry to disturb you at this hour..." Beth began.

"Hour?" echoed Mr Culpeper, stroking his long white beard distractedly. He looked up from his work and out through the window. "Oh, hour, yes..."

"It's just that we need to see Ralph," John explained. "Urgently."

"Yes, yes," the herbalist muttered as he reached for a dusty jar of dried purple leaves and peered intently at some tiny writing on the label.

Beth caught John's eye and nodded towards the door at the back that led to the stairs. They both made their way through the shop, and Culpeper paid no heed to them. Ralph lived in a single chamber above the shop. He'd been recruited as a spy by Strange while he'd been plying his "trade" as a petty criminal. Yet despite his rough-and-ready existence, he was a loyal friend and an admirable – and mostly law-abiding – spy.

Ralph's door stood slightly ajar, and they could see there was no light inside.

"He will not be happy…" John said.

"'Tis his bad luck!" Beth pushed the door open and went to Ralph's bedside, where she gently tapped his shoulder.

He gave a sniff, groaned "Whaaa?" and turned to face away from them.

"Ralph!" John said impatiently. "We need your help!"

"We haven't got time for this – it's not long until eight o'clock," said Beth. She grabbed the blanket that was covering the boy and threw it back, revealing two spindly white legs sticking out of a crumpled blue and white striped nightshirt.

"Hey!" Ralph cried. He looked up, suddenly alert – his spy training kicking in. He sprang out of the bed and eyed Beth and John warily, ready to defend himself.

"It's us!" Beth said. "We've work to do. Groby's back, and something's happened to John's sister. We must act fast."

Ralph rubbed his eyes, panting hard. "You might have said so." He turned to John. "Something's happened to your sister? Groby?"

John nodded grimly. "And there's another plot against the King afoot. We'll tell you the story later, but we need to get to Pirates' Dock. We just don't know where it is."

"Blow me, and you a Navy Board man…"

"Never mind that. Can you tell us how to get there?"

"I can do better than that," Ralph said. "Find me boots, and I'll take you there."

They were heading back east, and the day's temperature was already rising. At first they followed the Thames, but then Ralph took them on a short cut inland to miss a lengthy bend in the river. Beth realized they were travelling along the Ratcliffe Highway, haunt of highwaymen and cut-throats of the kind even Edmund Groby might hesitate to tangle with. They were approaching one particularly shady-looking alehouse when the door burst open. A group of rough-looking men staggered out into the road in an eruption of coarse laughter, swearing and shouting. One of the men immediately fixed his eyes on John.

"What you lookin' at?"

John was about to answer, but Ralph quickly jumped in. "You seen Jack Wood in there, mate?"

The surly man turned his unsteady gaze on Ralph. "Jack Wood? What's it to you?"

"Oh, just supposed to be meetin' up with him tonight, that's all."

The man seemed to be giving the matter some thought, as if seeing things in a new light. "No, I ain't seen Jack Wood."

One of the other men grabbed his arm and pulled him away. "Come on, Ben. They're a waste of time!"

He took one last surly look at them, and then accompanied his friends on their teetering journey to the next inn.

"Who's Jack Wood?" John asked.

"He's the guv'nor in these parts. You don't mess with his friends."

John was impressed. "You're a friend of the toughest man on the Ratcliffe Highway?"

"Lord, no. I stay well clear of him. But *they* didn't know that, did they?"

It was typical Ralph, and Beth couldn't help laughing. But just when her uneasiness about travelling along this notorious thoroughfare was beginning to melt away, Ralph began to lead them down a series of alleys towards the river. Each one seemed to be narrower and darker than the last. The smells and voices, and half-visible figures lounging in doorways, had the three of them huddling together as they picked their way through the potholes, rotting debris and scurrying rats. Eventually Beth caught sight of the fast-flowing water of the Thames glistening in the morning sun and they emerged onto a dockside.

And nailed to the side of a ramshackle wooden building, Beth saw a weather-beaten, crudely carved sign:

EXECUTION DOCK

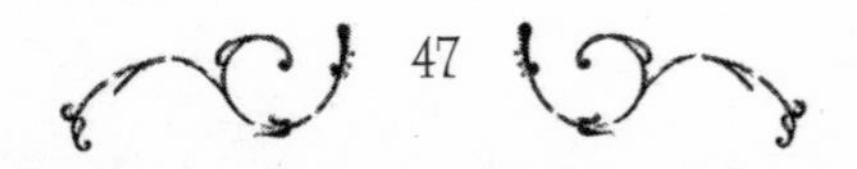

Chapter Five

Ultimatum

"But we're supposed to be at *Pirates'* Dock," said John irritatedly, eyeing the ominous sign.

It was low tide, and in the mud on the shore Beth saw a rectangular wooden frame made from two stout posts, with a crossbar joining them across the top. From the centre of the crossbar hung a frayed, mouldy length of rope, flapping in the breeze.

"That's where they hang 'em," Ralph told them in an unusually solemn voice. "The proper name might be Execution Dock, but round here it's known as Pirates' Dock. When they catch 'em, they rope 'em up there and

leave their bodies 'til three tides have washed over 'em. Not a pretty sight by then, believe me – but it sends a message to the rest, see?"

John swallowed, and despite the muggy heat Beth felt a shiver run through her. Then she remembered they were here for a purpose, and time was short. She surveyed the scene around her. At the water's edge stood two tall wooden cranes for loading and unloading goods from ships, and across the wharf were two imposing warehouses. There was no sign of anyone, and the whole area was quiet as the grave.

"At least it looks like we've got here before them," John said.

"Yes," Beth agreed. "You get ready for them, John. Ralph and I can find a place to hide where we can see what's going on when they arrive."

"Haven't played hide-and-seek for years!" said Ralph.

There was enough soft morning light for Beth to see along the river to the next wharf. She looked over some barrels on the edge of the quay, but soon realized that if the kidnappers came by river she would be too close and might be spotted. But beyond the barrels, Beth noticed some rope dangling from a rusty iron mooring ring bolted to the edge of the wharf. The rope from the

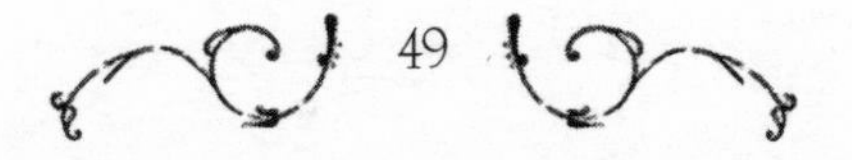

scaffold was old and rotten, but this looked new.

"Come and look at this!"

Ralph came across and took in the scene, then peered over the edge of the quayside. "And there's marks," he said. There were grooves in the mud that looked as though they'd been made by a keel.

"They're recent," John noted.

Ralph nodded. "As soon as the tide comes in and goes out again them marks'll be washed away. Someone's had a small boat, maybe a rowing boat, moored here within the last few hours. Could have been the kidnappers, scoping it out for a meeting point."

"Could well have been…" Beth replied. She looked up at the sky. Orange fingers of sunlight were feeling their way across the roofs of the houses. "We'd better take cover. It must be nearing eight o'clock."

Beth and Ralph quickly went their separate ways in search of hiding places and vantage points. They left John standing alone on the dockside, waiting for the people who had taken his sister captive.

* * *

Beth tugged the top of her shirt up over her mouth and nose to try and keep out the intense, stomach-churning stench. The little shack in front of the main warehouse must have once been used to store fish, but whoever had last cleaned it out hadn't done a very good job. It gave her a good view of the dock, though, and she should be just within earshot when the kidnappers arrived. She couldn't see Ralph through the crack in the wooden walls of her hiding place. He had made himself invisible, but she knew he was lying flat inside a small boat that was raised up on beams on the wharf, awaiting repair. John himself stood at the edge of the dock, a lone figure gazing across the Thames. Beth imagined how she would feel if Maisie had been kidnapped, and seeing him standing there all alone she wished there was more she could do for him. Hopefully there soon would be.

For now, all she could do was wait, and keep swallowing back the waves of nausea. The dockside was bathed in sunlight, and the vapoury mist rising from the river told her that the day would be yet another hot one. Beth was on her hands and knees, shuffling around to ward off the growing sensation of cramp in her right thigh. She had been hiding for only about ten minutes, but it already felt like longer.

Suddenly she heard the sound of oars splashing in the water and saw John stiffen, focusing his attention on a particular spot along the river that she couldn't at first see. Soon, a long rowing boat glided into view carrying three occupants. Beth cursed inwardly when she realized they were all men – they hadn't brought Polly with them. The man at the front of the boat stood up as it drifted against the landing stage with a gentle bump. He grabbed the same new rope she'd seen earlier, and used it to moor his craft.

As he stepped off the boat, Beth saw that it was Groby.

"You and your friends have interfered with our plans for your glorious King twice already, young cur," he snarled at John. "But now we hold the ace."

"Where is she?" John shouted. "Where is my sister?"

"Where no one will find her! You thought you were so clever, Turner: lowly clerk at the Navy Board by day, a skulking, devious spy for the sinful Charles by night."

"My sister has nothing to do with that!" John growled through gritted teeth.

"Ha!" Groby laughed. "You should have thought about that before you decided to meddle in affairs that don't concern you. Well, it's ended in your dear sister being snatched from the streets like a stray dog to

be put down – which is just what will happen to her unless you—"

As soon as Groby uttered his threat to Polly's life, John sprang at him. Groby didn't flinch, didn't move a muscle to defend himself. The two men with him dashed forwards, one either side of their leader. One gripped John by the arm, easily holding him at bay with one hand. The other came up behind him, grasped his waist and held a gleaming dagger to his throat. Beth held a hand to her mouth to keep from gasping.

"We have your precious sister," said Groby calmly in his ugly, rasping tones, "and now we need to get to your precious King. Which is the *more* precious to you, eh, Master Turner? Now is the time to decide. I'm a very fair and reasonable man and I give you a free choice! The King or Polly."

John elbowed the man with the knife hard in the gut and managed to struggle free, but he was soon recaptured, with the knife-wielding thug laughing menacingly in his ear.

"Don't even try it, boy," he spat.

"Why should I believe you'd release my sister anyway? You know my duty of loyalty to the King," John panted. "What makes you think *anything* you say could get me

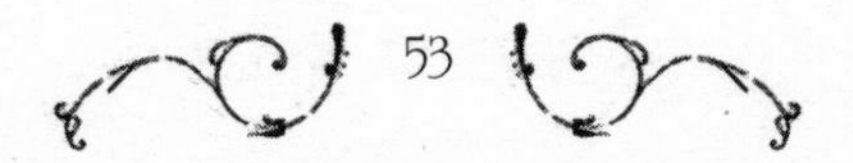

to betray him?"

Beth knew he was trying to be strong, and buying time to think, but she could hear John's voice shaking with stress.

"If you even stand a chance of seeing your precious young, innocent sister alive, you'll do as I say," Groby said, stepping closer to John. "Or would you prefer we gut you right here and try one of your other cohorts. That beautiful young girl-come-spy scum, perhaps?"

"All right," John interrupted quickly. "All right. I…" He sighed, and Beth's heart wrenched. "I *do* know how you can get to the King…"

"Oh, really?"

"Yes." John's voice was steadier now, and Beth felt a little more certain that he'd thought of a way to buy them more time. "The perfect opportunity. If you agree to let Polly go, I'll tell you not only where he'll be but also the exact spot you can lie in wait for him."

A slow smile spread across Groby's face. "Sounds almost too good to be true, Master Turner…"

John's jaw clenched. "That's because it *is* almost too good to be true. My job at the Navy Board means I'm privy to information about the King and his movements that few others are, and—"

He was interrupted by Groby's sneering cackle. "Oh, we're well aware of that, Master Turner. I have my spies too. Do you think it a coincidence that I have targeted *your* family? We know all about your clerkship at the Navy Board." His voice grew more ominous. "And we know there is to be a big new warship named in honour of the King and he is overseeing its construction. *You* are going to be our man on the inside."

The blood drained from John's face, and Beth felt just the same. John took a deep breath before he spoke again. "Before you get *any* help from me," he growled, "I want proof that my sister is still alive."

Beth found herself biting her lip as she waited for Groby's response. His shifty grey eyes narrowed and he rubbed his stubbly chin with his left hand, revealing the distinctive missing finger.

"If I keep my promise regarding the girl, then you will give me every single detail I need, and *you* will be the one to get us close to your King."

John's eyes narrowed angrily, and even without being able to see his face, Beth could tell he was fighting his emotions and trying to remain calm. She knew John wouldn't want to do anything to jeopardize their chances of getting Polly back – and somehow he'd also want to stop their plot against the King.

"Fine," John choked out. "Prove Polly is alive and I'll do what you say."

Groby waited a moment, then nodded to the man with the knife to John's throat. He lowered the weapon and withdrew to stand beside his leader.

"Give me two questions that only the girl would know the answer to."

John thought for a moment. "Our mother's favourite flower ... And a line from her favourite nursery rhyme."

"Very well. Proof that she is alive will be delivered to your house tonight, at which time you will tell me all the details we will need. You're going to get us so close to that royal rat, he won't know what's hit him 'til it's too late."

With that, Groby turned on his heels and returned to his boat, quickly followed by his henchmen.

Chapter Six

Blackwell Yard

Beth emerged quickly from her hiding place as soon as Groby's boat was out of sight.

"That's it," John said forlornly, head bowed. "We have no idea where they are holding her. I don't know what to do. It sounds … It sounds like I'll have to betray the King just to keep her alive."

"That's if he keeps his word and *does* keep her alive," Ralph remarked, popping up from inside the boat.

"*Ralph!*" Beth scolded him. "We've still got time. We're going to try and do something, find out information that could help us."

"Oh, yeah? And where do we start?"

"He's right," John groaned, flopping down onto the timber base of a cargo crane that towered above them. "There must be plenty of Republican sympathizers in London who they could use to help hide her – and who's to say she's still even *in* London by now? We don't have any way of narrowing the search down." He rested his elbows on his knees and let his chin sink into his hands.

"Perhaps we do…" said Beth.

John was too dejected to respond, but Ralph brightened a little. "Yeah?"

"Didn't you notice that mark on the side of Groby's boat?"

He gave a dismissive wave of his hand. "It was just an oil stain or something."

Beth shook her head. "It was black, but it was a regular shape, not an accidental mark. It was a rectangle or square – and I also thought I saw a little circle below it."

"Hang on!" Ralph said suddenly. "A black circle below a square? That's the mark of Blackwall Yard. Biggest shipbuilding yard on the river, that place."

Now John had straightened up and some of the life had returned to his eyes. "You know it?"

"Done a few little jobs there to earn a penny or two. Not for a long time, mind, but I still know a lot of the men."

"Can you get us in?"

"Too right I can!"

"Then what are we waiting for?" Beth cried. "If we save Polly, we save the King!"

"Urgh … you stink!" Ralph said to Beth as they headed east towards the East India Dock area, where trading ships brought in their cargos of tea, spices, silks and other exotic goods.

"Charming!" said Beth. She had grown so used to the smell from the fish shack that had permeated her clothing that she had forgotten about it. But now Ralph mentioned it, it came back to her anew.

"It's not that bad," said John, quickly leaping to her defence. Beth was touched, but then she noticed him hiding a funny face.

"'Tis a new perfume, popular with all the London ladies," she said with a mischievous grin. "*Eau de Pilchard.*"

John wrinkled his nose, not disguising it this time. "I think I prefer your usual scent…"

"Right," Ralph said, ignoring them. "'Tis a fair old walk. Better get a move on."

The route took them through Shadwell, and John wanted to call in and see how his parents were holding up, but Beth and Ralph persuaded him to avoid Bloodbone Alley. There was a good chance that they would ask too many awkward questions about what they were up to.

When they finally reached the yard, Beth was dismayed by what she saw. It was clearly a huge site, but a high wall surrounded the whole place, and at the entrance there was a jostling mob of labourers seeking work. There didn't seem to be any way through.

"How on earth are we going to get in?" John asked.

"With a bit o' nerve and the gift of the gab!" Ralph called.

He led them round the outside of the mass of men pressing towards the main entrance, ignoring the shouts and curses and arguments about who had pushed in and who hadn't. Beth was already noticing sweaty, tough, unshaven men eyeing them suspiciously.

"Oi – where d'you think you're goin'?"

That was the first angry cry, and it soon became a

chorus as others cottoned on to what was happening. They were almost at the entrance now. There were six burly yard employees barking orders and roughly pushing job-seekers about in an effort to maintain order. Beth had to yank herself free from a man in the crowd who had made a grab for her sleeve, then one of the security men confronted Ralph.

"Get to the back, sonny!"

"We're not after work, mate! For a start, *he's* just a mate of mine, and *she's* a fishwife's daughter from Billingsgate, as you can tell from the smell of her..."

Beth bit back a retort and allowed Ralph to continue.

"And I'm an old friend of Erazmus Clarke, the foreman in Dock Three. I just need a quick word with him and then we'll be on our way."

The man's guarded expression softened a little. "You know Erazmus?"

"Little feller. Not much hair. Tends to spit at you when he says anything with an 's' in it. Never ask him what he had for breakfast is my advice, because his favourite is sausages!"

Beth was impressed by Ralph's guile. The man was smiling a little now and he had won him over completely.

"In yer go – but ten minutes only, mind, or I'll come

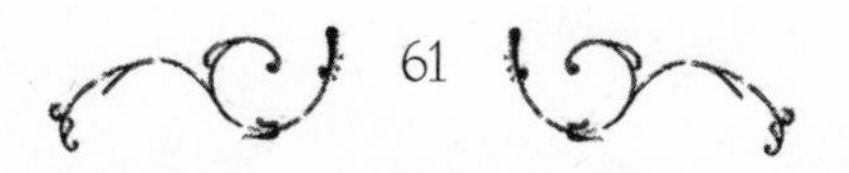

looking for yer!"

They were ushered in through the big main gates, happy to be immune from the howling protests of the mob.

The Blackwall Yard was as big and as full of bustle as a small town. The smell of fresh sawdust and tar hung in the air. People moved between the numerous buildings carrying tools and timber, and the sounds of sawing and hammering echoed from workshops small and large dotted around the site. Several slipways led down to the river, some with half-built ships like skeletons at the top, supported by a complicated framework of timber scaffolding. Ralph led them through the maze of lanes and open spaces with confidence; past a sail-making building that looked as big as St Paul's, a covered ropewalk that was narrow but just seemed to go on for ever…

A carpenter with his tool bag slung over his shoulder recognized Ralph as he was passing.

"Not back here working, you young scamp?" he called out.

"Nah. Just off to Dock Three for a quick chinwag with Mister Clarke."

"Well you won't find him there. He's at the Big House

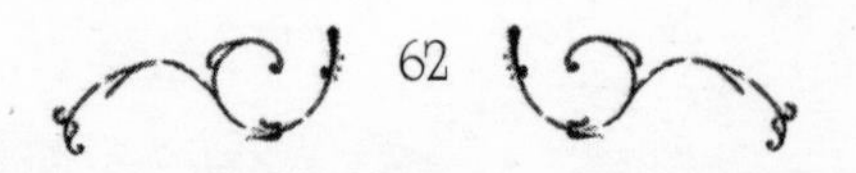

seeing Mister Perry."

"Cheers, matey."

"What's the Big House?" Beth asked Ralph as he headed them off in a different direction, away from the river.

"It's where Francis Perry lives, the man who owns this whole place."

The "Big House" was certainly quite grand for a dockyard, Beth thought, but pretty plain compared to the better houses in London. She was wondering how they were going to get past the servants when two men emerged from the front door and shook hands before parting.

"Erazmus!" Ralph cried.

Ralph's old boss seemed pleased to see him – but not so Francis Perry, the yard owner.

"I thought you were locked up," he grunted.

Ralph was undaunted. "That was *ages* ago, Mister Perry – and I've kept me nose clean ever since."

Perry eyed him up and down. "Not getting caught isn't the same as not thieving in the first place. I can't give you any work here – there's enough things go missing as it is. Besides, you've seen all the men outside. People have come in from miles around since we got that new contract, and—"

"No, no, Mister Perry. I ain't looking for work. I've just come to ask about a rowing boat."

"Eh?"

"Quite a long one, clinker-built with red lines painted round the tips of the oars and the Blackwall mark on the gunwales. We saw one at Pirates' Dock not long back with your mark on and we thought we'd pop along and see if, as a friend, you might be able to do us a deal on her to hire. Bit short of a few bob at the moment you see…"

Beth could tell from Perry's reaction that Ralph's description had hit a nerve. He tried to hide it, but a sudden extra alertness had come into his eye and he was suddenly more guarded.

"It's not for hire. It's just something the men use to go here and there on the river – that'll be why you saw it at Pirates' Dock. Probably gone to take some trenails. They're always running out."

"Ah, right…" Beth could tell that Ralph didn't believe him either.

"Who are your friends, anyway?"

Perry had hitherto barely noticed Beth and John, but since the mention of the boat he had taken a sudden interest in them, studying their faces closely.

"Oh," Ralph replied nonchalantly, "this here is Perriwinkle, a simple-minded lad who I look after. And the girl is his sister Betsey. Sorry for the whiff about her – she works with her mother, who's a fishwife at Billingsgate."

Beth clenched her jaw in irritation but managed to maintain an innocent expression. She saw that John was trying hard to do so as well.

Perry's eyebrows furrowed deeply and he appeared about to question Ralph further before thinking better of it. "Hmm. Well I can't help you with a boat and I'm a very busy man, so perhaps it's best you go." With that, he turned his back on them and headed back into the Big House.

"He wasn't telling us everything," said John, as they trudged back the way they'd come.

"You think I don't know that?" Ralph said.

"But he knows something about the boat, and Polly's life is at stake. We can't just walk away and forget about it!"

"I agree he knows something," said Beth. "Ralph's done the right thing. If we make him more suspicious than he already is, he'll only report everything we say back to whoever's behind it."

"But the boat's our *only* clue!" John smacked his fist into the palm of his other hand in frustration. Beth knew he was only thinking of his sister, and she wanted to tell him everything would be all right. The problem was, she was no surer of that than he was.

"Wait!"

It was Erazmus Clarke, hurrying to catch them up. They were outside some sort of big shed from which emanated the sound of timber being sawn in a steady rhythm. He nodded his head and led them round the corner of this building to a quieter spot.

"Look, 'tis only a boat, so for the life of me I don't know what all the cloak and dagger stuff is about. I'm telling you this because you're a good lad at heart, Ralph, and I don't want anything to happen to you."

"What do you mean?"

Erazmus lowered his voice to a whisper. "A couple of men turned up at the yard yesterday to see Mister Perry about taking a boat like the one you mentioned. Perry asked me to take them to the boat, but there was just something a bit off about them. One said something to the other about needing to hurry up so they could 'move the package'."

John, Ralph and Beth all looked at each other, and

Beth knew they were all thinking the same thing. They might have been talking about Polly…

"They just seemed … shifty," Clarke continued. "I recognized one of them and said so, but he seemed even more anxious when I did."

"Was he short and swarthy – perhaps with a finger missing from his left hand?" asked Beth.

"No. It was a fellow I've seen here before, as I say. We've done some work on the royal barge and he's been down here dealing with the paperwork a couple of times—"

"Royal barge?" John echoed.

"He's a servant at Somerset House, where Queen Henrietta lived after Charles I was executed. Hewer, his name. Ed Hewer."

"Did you overhear anything more these men said? Is there anything else you can tell us?" Ralph pressed him.

Just then a workman passed the building whose shadow they were standing in and glanced their way. Clarke gave him a casual nod, and the man walked on seemingly uninterested in their little rendezvous.

"I've got to get back to work. All I can say is I don't know what's going on and I don't want to. For God's sake, be careful!"

* * *

"We need to contact Strange," said John as they left Blackwall Yard. "He ought to know about all this, and he might know what we should do next."

"*We* know what we should do next," said Ralph, dabbing his sweaty brow. His gold earring flashed in the blazing sun. "Go to Somerset House and find this Ed Hewer feller."

"I think John's right," Beth said. "A lot's happened since we last saw Strange, he should be brought up to date. If Hewer is linked to Groby, then Alan Strange may well know about him. I suppose it makes sense to…" Her attention was suddenly drawn to the river. "How come there are so many boats coming this way?"

Ralph and John followed Beth's gaze, and all three came to a halt. As they were headed west back towards London, dozens of small craft loaded with people and belongings were coming down river towards them.

"Well I never," said Ralph, scratching his head. "It's like some sort of crazy race the way they're going at it – but it's far too hot for that if you ask me."

"I don't think it's a race," said John. "This reminds me of a story my grandfather told me."

They had stopped near Old Swan Stairs, one of the many landing stages along the banks of the Thames. Boats of all types were jostling to tie up at the few mooring places so that their passengers could disembark with their things. A man from one of the first boats to reach the stairs came struggling up, sagging under the strain of his precarious load. He carried a rolled-up carpet, various items of clothing, a small wooden chest and a large ball of cheese.

"What's happening, sir?" Beth asked.

The sweat-soaked, terrified man just hurried past them as if unaware of their presence.

John answered for him. "Fire! There was a big fire about thirty years ago and my grandfather saw scenes just like this. I thought he must have been exaggerating – 'til now."

Beth sniffed the air. "Goodness. I think I can smell it…"

Ralph sniffed too. "Well, I can't. There's always fires in London with all the houses being made of wood. No need for a panic like this. We must keep moving!"

Beth looked at John, and they both nodded. "There are plenty of people who can take care of a fire," she said. "We have a more important matter to attend to."

But as soon as they approached the Tower of London there was no longer any doubt about the smell of burning. From the top of Tower Hill they saw a great pall of smoke hanging over the city, its ominous blue-black colour interrupted by the occasional tongue of flame rising high into the air. They could hear voices now too. Beth thought they sounded like a big fairground in the distance – except the cries they could hear were not ones of joviality, but alarm and terror.

"Wrong way!" a woman shouted to them from a boat, clutching a screaming baby in her arms while her husband rowed for all he was worth. "Don't go that way – the whole city will soon be ablaze!"

Ralph hesitated. Even in the harsh sunlight and dazzling blue sky, they could now see an orange glow above the rooftops.

John didn't stop. "We must carry on! We *must*!"

There was a dry, hot breeze at their backs and it was strengthening. "Come on, Ralph," Beth urged, "before the wind stokes the fire. Let's at least see what we can do."

They skirted Seething Lane, which was near where John worked at the Navy Board, and found themselves on the outskirts of the City, forcing their way against the tide of people fleeing the flames. They scattered as a man and woman barely clinging to a spooked, wild-eyed horse came bolting down the centre of Eastcheap. Struggling through the growing crowds, Beth became temporarily parted from John and Ralph. Forcing her way through the throng, she finally caught up with them at the corner of Eastcheap and Pudding Lane.

A sudden gust of wind sent sparks and flaming debris flying across the street from a blazing house. They landed like snowflakes of fire on top of a so-far untouched house, and within seconds fire rippled across the bone-dry roof. Within a couple of minutes, a sheet of flame had closed off Pudding Lane completely. Beth could feel the heat scorching her cheeks, and her nose was assailed by the acrid smell of burning wood, tar and fabrics.

"There ain't no way through that lot," said Ralph. "Looks like one o' them pictures of Hell."

"Not to St Paul's, maybe," John agreed. "But Somerset House is on the river. That's where your man said Hewer worked."

"One problem, though. The King's mother lives there," Ralph pointed out. "How would we get past the guards?"

"She doesn't live there any more," said Beth. "She left

for France last year. There are just a few noblemen and staff left now. Perhaps we can go by water."

They took one last look at the bonfire that had once been Pudding Lane, and turned back towards the Thames.

Chapter Seven

Somerset House

At Queenhithe Stairs, Ralph spotted a waterman returning from downriver with an empty boat. This landing stage was so close to the fire that most people were rushing past it to get transport further along the river, and there happened to be no one about at that moment.

"Anyone got any money?" he asked.

"I have," said Beth.

"Me too," said John.

They scrambled down the hill just as the waterman was tying up. He was lean, with the knotty, muscular

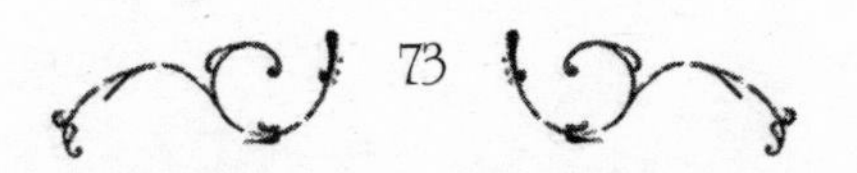

arms of all watermen, but Beth could see from his drooping posture and haggard face that he must already have made numerous trips. She paid him as they all clambered aboard the flat-bottomed lighter, usually used to transport people and goods to and from moored ships. The boatman took up his oars with a weary sigh and began to row east.

"No, not that way!" John cried.

"What yer mean, not that way? The fire's headin' *that way*, safety's *that way*," he said, using his thumb to direct them in case they were in any doubt.

"But we want Somerset House," said Beth. "We, uh, we live near there and we must go and help our families."

The waterman shrugged and began to pull on the starboard oar to turn the boat about. "Maybe the fire'll get that far, maybe it won't; but it's the worst I've ever seen. Suit yerselves."

"Somerset House itself wouldn't burn, would it?" John asked him. Beth could tell he was worried Polly was being held there.

The waterman shook his head. "Made o' stone like a lot of them grand places along the riverfront. But what with people hurryin' and scurryin' everywhere, won't be easy to find your folks."

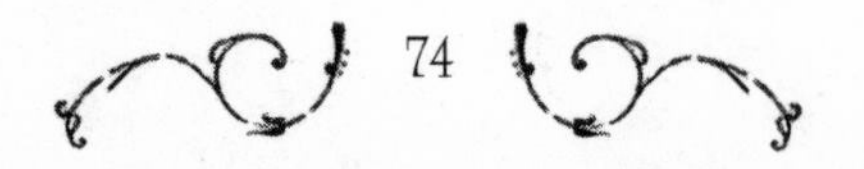

"We'll find who we're looking for," Beth assured him. She hoped she was right.

They finally pulled alongside Somerset House, and the waterman dropped them off opposite the magnificent building. Its pale stone looked strangely serene against the clear summer sky, while just along the river warehouses were burning to the ground.

Beth led John and Ralph up the slope and into the manicured garden. Through the windows she could see people moving about, but not evidently in a great panic. People this far from the fire probably didn't realize how serious it was yet. However, they must have been taking precautions, because the main door facing the river was wide open. Servants kept emerging laden with personal belongings, adding to a growing pile by the steps.

The three crouched down behind a bush and watched for a moment.

"The next time someone goes back indoors, you two follow them and try to blend in – help with moving things outside," said Beth. "Get talking to people, see if anyone knows where to find Ed Hewer. I'm going to try to make my way down to the kitchens – cooks are always the first to hear the gossip."

"Someone's bound to realize we don't belong here,"

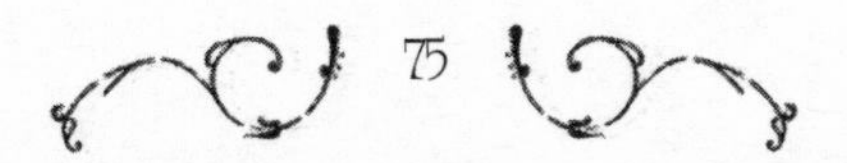

John said cautiously.

"I'm sure you can come up with a cover story."

They waited for a couple of minutes, then a young maid came out and deposited some neatly folded lace curtains on top of the pile before going back inside.

"*Now!*" Beth urged them. Ralph and John sprang from their hiding place and followed the girl into the house. Beth was close on their heels, and once inside she paused to take stock of the layout. Somerset House was like a cathedral inside, easily the biggest and most impressive place she'd ever been in. She was in a spacious hallway, and there were colourful murals on the lofty ceilings. Ahead of her was a magnificent double staircase sweeping up to the next floor, but it was what was behind the stairs that interested Beth: small, insignificant doors on either side. In places like this, the doors used by owners and their guests were designed to make a statement. They were invariably big and imposing. Those solely for the use of servants were smaller with little doorknobs and no fancy carvings – just like the one she could see in the shadow of the staircase.

Making sure the coast was clear, Beth ran across the hall – taking a slight detour along the way to hitch up her skirts and empty the contents of a large bowl of fruit

on a little side table into them – and went through the door on the right. She found herself in a narrow, dark corridor with a door on either side at the end of it. She listened behind the first one and, hearing no signs of life, quietly opened it. What she saw brought a broad grin to her face. It was a sort of storeroom, where food from the kitchens below was kept before being taken into the dining room. What particularly caught her eye was more fruit in a basket, just like the sort she carried herself when she used to sell oranges at the theatre.

She added the fruit from her skirts to it, then, picking up the basket, went to listen at the other door. She could smell baking bread – a good sign – but then she heard footsteps coming up what must have been a flight of stairs behind the door. She had to think fast, and instead of waiting and looking suspicious, she threw open the door and began to boldly descend the stone steps, pretending not to notice the servant girl who was coming up them.

"Ooh, sorry darlin' – didn't see you there."

The young girl, wearing a flour-stained blue apron, was initially lost for words. "Are … are you supposed to be down here? Cook's very particular…"

"Supposed, luv? Supposed?" said Beth in her broadest Cockney accent. "I'd be in trouble if I *weren't* goin' down

there. You all needs yer energy, don't yer?"

"Energy? For what?"

"When the fire comes!"

The girl gasped. "Is it really coming this way? They were saying it should soon be put out…"

"Put out? There ain't no putting *that* fire out, darlin'. Won't be long before it reaches 'ere, and you need to be ready. Lots o' work to do, and they sent me to see yer well provided for."

"Who did?"

"Why, the Lord Mayor and 'is officers! Ordered all the orange-sellers to go out and provide sustenance for the poor folk fleein' the fire."

The servant now seemed suitably alarmed, so Beth stood to one side and allowed her to hurry past. The stairs took her directly into the kitchen. She expected people to turn and stare at her, but instead the cook was bawling out orders and everyone was busy preparing for what looked like a sumptuous meal. Despite the initial preparations for evacuation upstairs, down here it seemed life was carrying on as normal.

"Oranges! Who'll take my juicy oranges?" Beth announced, but it was a rather tentative cry. In the hubbub of the kitchen, with the cook barking orders to

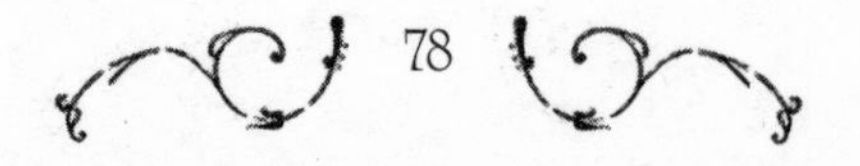

her deputies, and her deputies yelling at the skivvies, no one even took any notice of her. Then she remembered the lessons in voice projection she'd received from William Huntingdon.

"ORANGES! DON'T BE SHY – COME AND GET 'EM! RIPE AND JUICY!"

"Somebody get that cheeky wench out of my kitchen," growled the cook without looking up from her work. A young man who had been skinning rabbits dropped a bloody carcass on the table and shuffled hesitantly towards her. He was no older than her, and the closer he got the less sure of himself he seemed.

Beth shook out her long, chestnut-brown hair and flashed her green eyes at him. "*This* is where they keep all the good-lookin' ones, then!"

Heat instantly came to the boy's cheeks, and he seemed uncertain of whether to smile or try to look stern.

"Cook doesn't like people in her kitchen that don't belong," he mumbled.

"Don't belong?" Beth exclaimed. "Me and you belong together, that's what I thought as soon as I saw yer." She grinned. "These oranges has been sent special, like – here, take one!" She picked one from her basket and held it out to him.

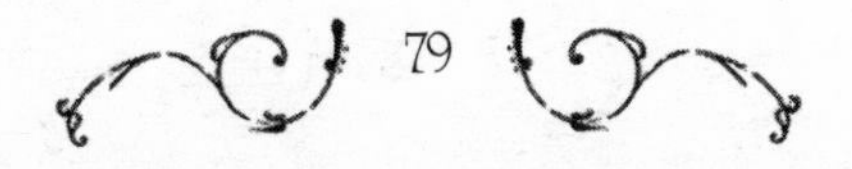

He had half an eye on Beth while glancing in Cook's direction, seemingly at a loss as to what to do next. The cook didn't *appear* to be paying them any attention, but when it became apparent that her reluctant ejector wasn't getting anywhere, she abruptly stopped what she was doing and turned on Beth.

"Does this place *look* like a theatre, missy?" She was tall, almost Beth's height, with a strong, jutting chin. Not as stout as Big Moll, but still big-framed. She had a gruff look about her but, Beth sensed, a gleam of humour never far from her eye.

"No, no, I've 'ad my fill o' them places!"

"Then what, may I ask, are you doing in here?"

"The Lord Mayor sent me."

"Oh yes? Well, the King told me to tell you to hop it. I'm not going to tell you again—"

"'Tis true!" Beth protested. "'Tis to do with the fire."

"The fire near the Bridge? What's that got to do with orange-sellers?"

"Well, when it gets 'ere you're all gonna be too busy to eat, but you'll need to keep your strength up. The Mayor thought oranges might be just the thing."

"And I bet he's making a tidy profit out of them!"

"No – they're free. He made it quite plain, bless 'im.

'I'll not profit from my people in times of distress' was his exact words."

By now the cook was looking more puzzled and apprehensive than angry. "Distress? The fire by the Bridge? How big is it, then? Is it really spreading as the rumours say?"

By now work in the kitchen had almost ground to a halt as people who had overheard the talk of fire began to gather round.

"What with the 'ot summer dryin' everythin' out, and now the wind blowin' the sparks all over the place, it don't seem like nobody can do nothin' to stop it, missus. And that wind is bringin' it this way!" Beth said dramatically.

Cook rolled her eyes. "Typical. This place has just gone down and down since dear old Henrietta went to France. She stayed on here after they chopped the old King's head off, may the Lord bless him, and she was very good to me..." She paused to wipe a tear from her eye.

"So who lives here now?" Beth pressed.

"Royal hangers-on, and I don't mind who hears me say it. Oh, they all go by fancy titles: Lord this and Sir that, but none of them can hold a candle to Her Majesty. Only interested in squandering their money on

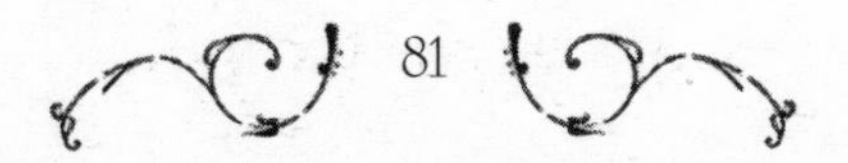

fancy clothes and parties like the one we're supposed to be having tonight. They're out playing Pell Mell while London burns!"

"Well," said Beth, "I'm not sure 'ow long it'll take the fire to come this far – but all I *can* say is I reckon there'll be plenty of roasted stuff on the menu! I just hope Ed's safe..."

"Ed?"

"Oh, Ed Hewer. Friend o' my brother. Last I 'eard he was workin' here but maybe 'e's moved on...?"

"Oh, *him*. No, he's still Lord Cumbria's manservant but he's not here at the moment. His master's one of them out playing Pell Mell on the Strand, would you believe?"

"Ah. Maybe I'll bump into him on my way home, then," Beth replied as casually as possible. As soon as she had finished giving the staff of Somerset House their own oranges, Beth went back upstairs to find John and Ralph. The pile of belongings had turned into three piles by now. It seemed the news of the fire was spreading – the smell of it was now clearly in the air, even here. She found her friends helping to transfer heavy strong-boxes, presumably containing money and valuables, into a coach with an ornate coat of arms emblazoned on its

door. She hung around until no one else was around, and then pulled John aside.

"Find anything out?"

"They seem to be mostly royalist supporters here, so it's an odd place to find a republican spy," he said.

"But if you're a republican spy," said Ralph, sidling up to join them after depositing some silver candlesticks in the coach, "you'd *want* to be among royalists! Good disguise, isn't it?" He glanced back at the expensive items yearningly, but Beth shook her head warningly.

"The upper crust certainly weren't taking the fire seriously, at least not at first," said John. "A servant was sent out not long after it started to see what it was all about and heard the Lord Mayor say a young boy could pee it out!"

"They'll worry soon enough," Beth said, looking at the black pall of smoke in the east. "But I've been doing my own snooping – and I know where we can find Ed Hewer."

Chapter Eight

Hewer's Secret

"Good strike, sir!"

Beth, John and Ralph observed the Pell Mell players keenly from a short distance away. The speaker was a man wearing a shiny auburn wig and a resplendent blue velvet coat trimmed with fine white lace. A prominent belly stretched his waistcoat to its very limits, yet his silk breeches revealed a pair of surprisingly skinny legs.

"Thank you, Cumbria. But I've taken eight hits to your six so I must improve my game if I'm to win." The portly man's opponent was just as finely attired, taller, and wore a black wig. He wore a chunky gold ring on his little finger with a large diamond in its centre that glinted in the sunlight. The men each had a sort of long wooden mallet and a small wooden ball that they were hitting between hoops at either end of their course.

"I've seen this played in St James's Park," said John. They were standing in the shadows of an alley between Somerset House and the building beside it, trying to look as unobtrusive as possible as they watched. "I've always thought it looked quite fun…"

"Can't see the point meself," Ralph remarked sniffily.

"'Tis whoever can hit their ball to the far end, through the hoop, then back again and through the other hoop in the fewest hits," John said obliviously.

"Lord Cumbria is obviously losing, then," said Beth. "But at least we know who he is. Now we just have to wait and see which of the servants attends to him, and we'll have Ed Hewer."

One of the two servants accompanying the two noblemen up the course was a wiry, angular young man with sharp features and lank fair hair. Ralph put his wager on this being Hewer, and Beth agreed. The game came to a premature end when Cumbria's ball rolled into a pile of horse dung by the side of the road, and he simply laughed, turned his back on it and walked away.

As the two players sauntered back to Somerset House, the manservants hurried to their masters' sides and took the mallets. The wiry, sharp-featured young man took Cumbria's.

Ralph grinned. "See – that's our man! You two stay here a minute. I reckon if I have a quick chat I'll soon get what we need out of him."

"Are you sure you should do it?" John said anxiously.

"Yeah! Trust me, I know these types of servants. They may seem lah-di-dah, but they're usually closer to my sort of background really. I'm pretty sure I'm the best one to relate to someone like Hewer…"

"Be careful, Ralph!" Beth warned. "If he's been dealing with Groby he may well have been warned about us."

Ralph waved her fears away dismissively. "This'll be a breeze!" He put his hands in this pockets and wandered over to Hewer, who was delicately picking the ball out of the horse dung while everyone else returned indoors.

Ralph tutted, causing Hewer to look up from his unpleasant task. "We get landed with all the best jobs, don't we?"

"Eh?"

"Oh, I'm the Earl of Coddingham's manservant. He once dropped a gold sovereign into his chamber pot, and

guess who he made fish it out?"

"Earl of Coddingham? Not sure I've heard of him." Hewer retrieved the ball and wiped it on his sleeve tentatively.

"Yorkshire man. Not all that fancy, and he don't get to London often. Anyway, he's gone drinking in Southwark, so he's given me the morning off."

"Ah," said Hewer, straightening his sinewy body up and holding out his hand. "Edward Hewer, manservant to Lord Cumbria."

Ralph looked at the hand and pulled a face. "Don't mean to appear rude…"

Hewer let it drop to his side, smiling sheepishly. "Oh, yes. Anyway, well met, uh…?"

"Yates," Ralph lied smoothly. "So, what's yours like for wages?"

"Not very generous," Hewer said, pursing his lips.

"Mine neither, considering all the hours they make us work – and the dirty jobs they give us!"

Hewer laughed.

"But," continued Ralph, "there's ways you can improve your lot, shall we say…"

Hewer scratched the side of his nose, leaving a dirty smear there. "How d'you mean?"

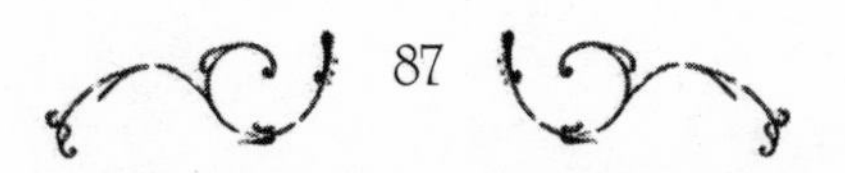

Ralph dropped his voice conspiratorially. "Well, only last night I was talking to a feller in the Duke's Arms, where we're staying. Turns out he's got a nice little scheme selling on his master's wine. The old boy is such a boozer he don't miss a bottle or two. This man says I can make meself at least three shillings if I want to be a temporary partner in the venture – maybe take some to sell back up north."

"Three shillings?" Hewer snorted. "I'm about to make as much money in a week as I could ever hope to earn in ten years!"

Ralph broke out in a smile. To Hewer it meant he was impressed, but inwardly Ralph was feeling smug. He knew the youth had taken his bait. "Oh, yeah? Do tell me more, friend."

"I wish I could bring you in on it, but it's not that kind of plan. See, I was approached by three men – right shady-looking bunch too – asking for a favour…"

"Sounds like an expensive favour."

Hewer looked around. "I shouldn't be telling you this," he whispered, "but turns out all they need is the use of a room. Well, there's loads of 'em in Somerset House since Old Henrietta left. The whole east wing's been shut up for over a year. So all I have to do is provide 'em with

a key, not notice any funny comings and goings, and *bang* – I'm a rich man!"

"Lucky devil! Look a bit villainous, do they, these men? Locals?"

"Look … I've said too much already. But one of 'em, lord! He's got a—"

"HEWER!"

They both spun round. Lord Cumbria was calling from the door of Somerset House.

"Better go. Nice meeting you, Yates. If I call into the Duke's Arms I'll buy you an ale."

Just as he was about to leave, a loud explosion rent the air, and then its shock wave echoed several times before it faded to nothing.

The two of them looked towards the City, where the dark smoke now bellowed skywards like a vast thundercloud.

"Someone's store of gunpowder's gone up in the fire," Ralph speculated. "Looks bad."

"Aye. Looks very bad."

Hewer hurried back into Somerset House, and Ralph took another glance back over his shoulder at the advancing fire. Shaking off the images it conjured, he ran back to Beth and John.

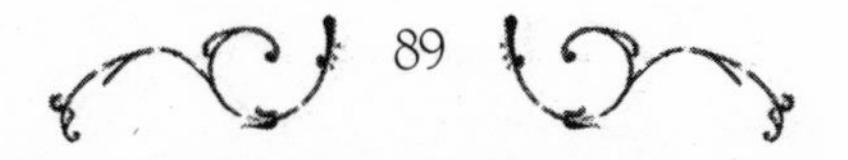

"He spilled the beans. I think I know where the kidnapper's base is..."

"Where?" John demanded urgently. "Where is it?"

Ralph turned his eyes on Somerset House, and the others followed his gaze. "You're lookin' at it."

Chapter Nine

Thoughts of Home

"What are we waiting for, then?" John said. "Let's go and investigate! Polly might be in there right now!"

Beth glanced at Ralph, and they both looked warily at their friend. "I know you want to look into this as quickly as possible," Beth said gently, "but it's getting too busy at Somerset House now. People are starting to panic about the fire, and we need to regroup and see if we can get in touch with Strange again. He might have received intelligence of his own alerting him to what's happening now, so he might be able to help."

John shook his head. "My sister's *life* is at stake—"

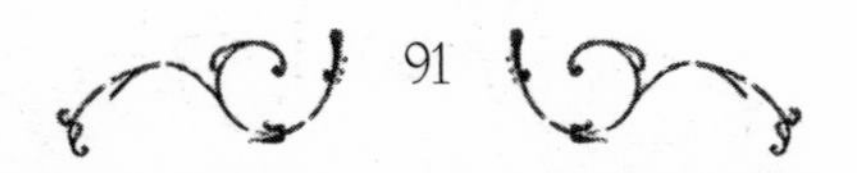

"We know," Beth said, resting a hand on her friends arm. She caught his gaze so that he could see she was sincere. "And we're going to do everything we can to get her back and stop Groby and his men. We just need to be careful."

"That's right," Ralph said, nodding. "We're going to—" His words disintegrated into a violent fit of coughing. A sudden gust of wind had brought a cloud of acrid smoke billowing along the Strand straight into their faces. They had to stop and turn their backs until it dissipated, and then Beth suddenly felt hands roughly brushing against her back.

"What are you doing?" she cried, spinning round. And then she saw – they all had tiny glowing specks on their clothes, sparks carried on the wind from the fire. She helped John and Ralph to brush them from their own clothing, and hurried on downwind. As they turned into Fleet Street, Beth could hardly believe the scene that met her eyes. It was like the crowds she had seen rushing to catch a glimpse of a royal procession – but this throng was not stampeding towards something, but away from it. Carts, carriages and horse riders crowded the centre of the road, with people on foot swarming around them like midges.

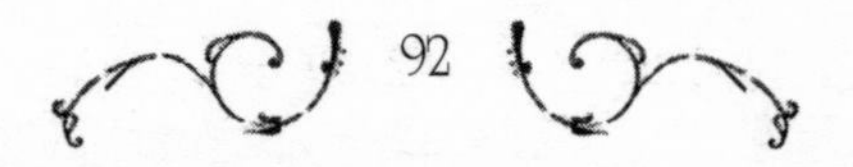

"That's Sir Richard Farmer!" Ralph exclaimed. He was looking at a man and woman still in their dressing gowns. They were riding a cart piled precariously high with wobbling chairs, tables and an assortment of other domestic items, all held in place with rope. Behind them came a very sickly-looking woman wrapped in blankets despite the heat, carried on a makeshift stretcher. Not long afterwards Beth spotted another invalid being moved to safety. This one was still actually in his sick bed, with four men at each corner struggling under the weight. To work their way against this tide of humanity Beth and the others had to flatten themselves against the walls and edge along crabwise. They could clearly see the flames in the distance above the rooftops now; the constant cracking of burning, splitting timbers sounded like an exchange of musket fire between two armies.

Ralph had taken the lead, but there was such a crush that Beth struggled to keep the back of his head in view as he dodged his way through the throng. However, when he bumped into someone coming the other way Beth immediately recognized the indignant voice of the aggrieved party.

"Out of the way, you little toad, or I shall take my stick to you!"

"You do and I'll land a tickler on your hooter, you miserable fat hog," came Ralph's retort.

"MISTER LOVETT!" Beth yelled above the din. She pressed forward, and now she could see not only Benjamin Lovett but William Huntingdon and some of the other players of the King's Theatre.

"Beth!" Huntingdon greeted her. "Going back to collect your belongings? Be quick – 'tis spreading mighty fast."

"It hasn't reached the theatre, has it?" she asked, aghast. It was not only the Drury Lane Theatre she was worried about but the Pie and Peacock where she lived with Maisie, which was close by.

"No, but it must only be a matter of time."

"How did it start?" John asked, distracted from his desire to go back to Somerset House by the chaos.

"They say 'tis something to do with Farrinor's bakery near the Tower."

"I heard t'was the perfidious French, and I do believe it to be so!" Lovett declared, his fleshy jowls wobbling with rage.

"Or the Dutch," Matthew, the theatre prompter added. "We are at war with both, after all, and they say this is just the start – first a fire to cause panic, then an

invading army to catch us while we are helpless!"

Beth glanced at Ralph and John, thinking of the conspiracies against the King. "Could it be true?"

"I know not, Beth," Huntingdon answered. "There is such a panic afoot and so many stories abroad that anything could be true. All I know is that the fire is spreading as fast as any invading army could, and that you must do whatever it is you have to do then leave. We are told people are gathering at Moorfields, beyond the city. Join us there if you wish…"

"Thank you, Mister Huntingdon. We'll be as quick as we can."

They said their goodbyes, and Beth, John and Ralph continued to battle their way east, where possible taking to alleys and side streets to avoid the worst of the crush. Beth felt for John and his missing sister, but there were other things pressing on her mind now and eventually she could contain herself no longer. She came to a halt and called to John and Ralph.

"I … I must go to Drury Lane and make sure Maisie is safe. I haven't forgotten about Polly, but we have some time. Groby said he would be back this evening with proof that she's safe, so until then…"

John patted her hand. "I understand. You're right that

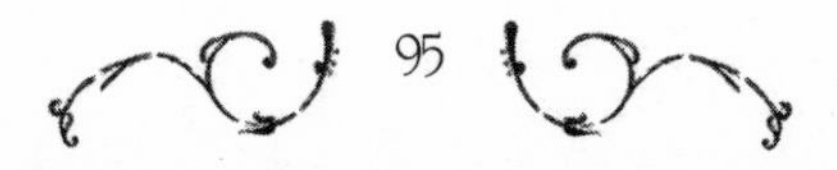

Somerset House will be too busy right now for us to investigate, and I should check on my family. This fire is looking worse than we thought. Ralph, you should see that your own lodgings and possessions are not in danger too. We can all meet up again in a couple of hours' time."

"Ain't hardly got no possessions to lose," Ralph replied matter-of-factly. "But I should like to see Mister Culpeper's all right. Weird old coot, but he's looked after me."

"Do what must be done then meet me back at Bloodbone Alley as soon as you can," John said. "Then we'll be ready for Groby."

They went their separate ways, Beth doubling back along Aldwych. She was pleased to see Drury Lane was so far untouched. But beyond the tower of St Paul's, which still rose majestically above the skyline of London, a sheet of flame and smoke rose. She could hear screams and shouts, creaking and thudding as buildings fell. But if the waterman thought Somerset House was safe, then surely the cathedral could withstand the raging fire?

"Beth!" cried Maisie, as soon as she walked through the door of the inn. "We were worried about you!" The younger girl came bounding up to Beth and threw her arms around her. "Have you been to see the fire? It won't

come this far, will it?"

"'Tis still spreading, but I hope it will burn itself out before it gets here."

Big Moll was pouring ale from a jug into the tankard of a man sitting at a corner table. She stopped and looked outside on hearing Beth's words. The panes in the window were opaque, like many of those in humbler buildings, but yellow and orange lights danced in strange patterns on the glass. "They say they're pulling houses down in its path to stop it – and there's the cathedral."

"Aye," said the old man she was serving with indifference, taking a swig from his beer. "Old Paul's gonna put a stop to that there fire." He wiped his mouth with his sleeve and got back to reading the news sheet by the light of the fire.

"But some say it's God's wrath," said Maisie. "Because we're all so sinful he's sent down a terrible punishment."

"People will always blame God when something goes wrong," said Moll, pushing her sleeves higher up her brawny arms and plonking the jug down on the bar. "I'd look closer to home before I did that. Like that baker on Pudding Lane and his smouldering ovens..."

* * *

Not knowing how far or fast the fire was spreading, Ralph decided to stick to the river bank as much as possible on his way to Black Swan Alley. He hurried down Middle Temple Lane, hoping to get some sort of boat, but every craft seemed to be already out on the water and the number of people waiting for their return was so great that he found himself trudging along the water's edge. The closer he got to London Bridge, the deeper his heart sank. The fire was moving through the streets like a raging monster. With a growing sense of unease, Ralph pressed on. He could see a boat stationed at Queenhithe Stairs, close to Walter Culpeper's shop, and someone throwing bundles of belongings wrapped in sheets into it. From his low riverside vantage point he could see flames ahead, but not how far they had reached. He grabbed the arm of a man carrying a great sack over his shoulder.

"Black Swan Alley!" he pleaded. "Has it got as far as Black Swan? Three Cranes?"

"And further," muttered the man before continuing on his way.

Ralph couldn't get close. The warehouses and coal wharves along the river bank were one mass of flame and stinking smoke. Even from fifty yards away the

heat made his face flush, and even though he saw the occasional gap he knew it would be impossible to pass through.

He tried going inland, skirting round the fire and coming to Black Swan Alley down New Queen's Street, which it hadn't yet reached, but that too proved impossible. He hurried to the highest point in the area, pushing through the tide of people carrying their belongings down to boats waiting on the river. It was a spot where he could see between the buildings towards his home – but he couldn't see the alley itself. All that was visible was a forest of leaping flames and the occasional black outline of a building. Old Walter Culpeper was a little deaf and couldn't get about as well as he used to.

Ralph closed his eyes and resorted to something he hadn't done for years. He prayed.

Chapter Ten

Kettles and Pans

"It *must* burn itself out soon!" Ralph groaned as they wended their way towards Cornhill through the fleeing crowds. He and Beth had met up once more while both on their way to Bloodbone Alley a couple of hours after they'd departed. He'd had to abandon his hopes of getting to Culpeper's, but with Beth's encouragement he still held out hope that the old man and his shop were all right. The warm wind had not dropped, however, and little sparks, burning slivers of wood and paper drifted above their heads.

They only got as far as the Royal Exchange. Looking

beyond it Beth saw a three-storey house engulfed in flames that were quickly spreading. She was a fair distance away, but still had to hold a hand in front of her face to ward off the heat. Then, without warning, there was a crack like a large gun being fired, and the overhanging top floor of the house toppled into the street. All the onlookers involuntarily jumped back. The whole building began to crumple now, with a horrific shrieking sound from the twisting and breaking timbers. There were urgent warnings to get back – this area was quickly becoming unsafe.

"The river!" shouted Ralph over the roar of the flames. "It's the quickest way."

The banks of the Thames were as busy as Cheapside on market day, but with an added layer of panic and desperation as people tried to get places in the few available craft.

"This doesn't seem real," said Beth. "'Tis like a dream."

"Nightmare, more like," said Ralph. "Blimey – hide your eyes, young lady!"

Despite the warning, Beth instinctively looked to see what Ralph had spotted. A man was clambering into a lighter, a pile of goods balanced precariously in his arms. He must have left his escape 'til the last minute,

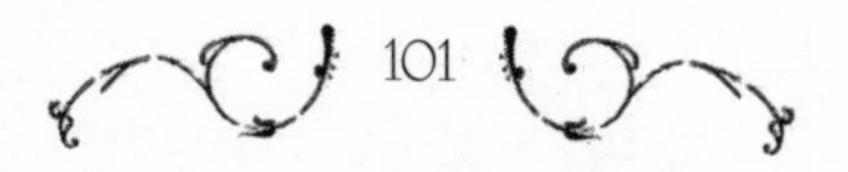

because the only thing that preserved his modesty was a sheet wound around his body. He'd obviously been so desperate to hold onto his possessions that he couldn't spare a hand to keep the sheet in place. In the scramble to get aboard it had slipped lower and lower – until it finally ended up floating in the river and the man was naked in the boat! Beth could see his pink bottom wobbling as he tried to keep his footing. A woman shrieked and a couple of men burst out laughing, the sound echoing across flowing waters that reflected the oranges, reds and yellows of the inferno. At least, she thought, there could be some humour amid all this horror…

Once they had gone beyond the Tower they finally left the fire behind, even though they could still hear and smell it. But at Bloodbone Alley, another strange sight met their eyes. Most of the people around here were out of their houses, many up trees and poles or even on roofs, watching the distant spectacle like an audience at a play. Beth and Ralph found that John was still indoors, though, silent and pale, awaiting news of Polly with his family. At their knock, he came outside to talk to them out of earshot.

"Nothing?" Ralph asked.

John shook his head. "What if she's not at Somerset

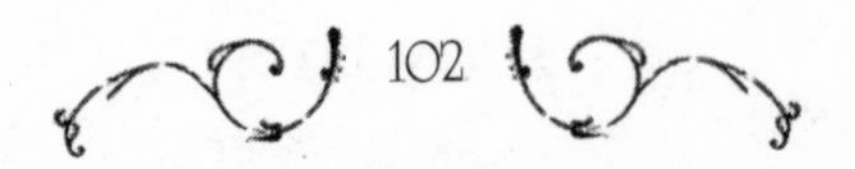

House? What if they'd been keeping her at a house that's now caught up in the middle of the fire? What if they fled and left her there? They must know she can't run, but I wouldn't put it past them to simply—"

"John, John…" said Beth resting a hand on his shoulder. "Polly is useful to them so I'm sure they'll want to keep her safe."

"That's right," Ralph agreed. "And we ain't seen no bodies nor heard of no deaths at all, and we've been right up to the fire."

"Has it reached St Paul's?" John asked.

"No," Beth replied. "It's only a matter of time – but surely it can't touch such a building as that?"

"Well, I didn't like the look of all that wooden scaffolding round it for the repairs…" said Ralph.

"It will burn, I'm sure of it," said John. "Then Strange will have no way of signalling to us. Why hasn't he made contact in some other manner? Does all this mean *nothing* to him?"

Beth gave his shoulder a reassuring squeeze. "It means something to *us*. We'll do all we can to find her. We'll stay up all night if necessary. Groby's men might be delayed by the fire, but I believe they'll come." She just hoped there was nothing in her voice that told John she

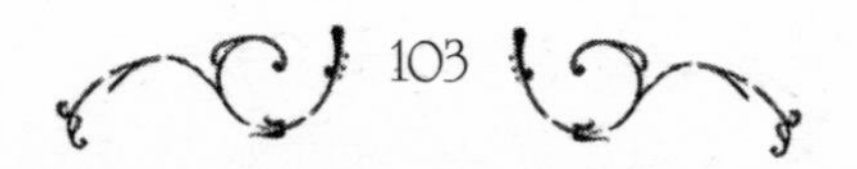

wasn't quite as optimistic as she was trying to sound. This fire had changed everything and turned London upside down. It could well be that Polly's safety was the last thing on the kidnappers' minds if they were caught up in it.

John sighed, and rubbed his brow. He looked sick with worry, obviously thinking the same thing. "I don't know. What if … what if I have no choice but to do as Groby asks? I have to do everything I can to save Polly. She's my sister – my *blood.* I know it's my sworn duty to protect the King, but what if—"

Beth's eyes widened in alarm as she cut him off. "No! Don't think like that, John. We're going to stop Groby. You can't let these conspirators get the better of you." She eyed him closely, but he just had a faraway look in his eyes. A look that worried Beth…

Once John's family had reluctantly retired to bed, John snuck Beth and Ralph in to wait for news with him. John sat in an uncomfortable-looking wooden chair by the door, while Beth and Ralph settled on two other chairs in the small room. There was some sporadic, whispered conversation at first, as Beth filled John in on what they'd seen of the fire on the journey to his house. But soon the words dried up and the three of them sat in

uneasy silence, bathed in candlelight and staring at the door, struggling to stay awake. Several times Beth felt herself nodding and jerking her head back up, checking to see if the others had noticed. The final time this happened, she turned to look at Ralph beside her and saw that he actually had drifted off, his chin resting on his chest. She couldn't help thinking how much younger and more innocent he looked when asleep.

Then she heard a sound that instantly snapped her into full wakefulness. It wasn't very loud, but the shuffling sound in the street was quite distinct. John must have heard it too, because his head swivelled towards the door. There was a brief silence, then three short, quiet knocks. Beth felt her heart quicken, and John leaped to his feet. By now Ralph had woken too.

The three of them quietly gathered at the door. John gripped the knob, steeled himself for a second, and then slowly opened it. Two men stood in the darkness.

"We have a message for John Turner," said one of the men softly, and John nodded. Beth could see his jaw clenching and unclenching with tension.

"You wanted proof that Polly was alive?" said the other.

The man with the soft voice said simply: "Violets.

Kettles and pans…"

"What are you on about?" Ralph grumbled. "Listen, mister, just tell us—"

"Say the bells of St Ann's," John murmured.

"What's going on?" Beth asked. She could see that John was now looking at least a little more relieved.

"Violets are our mother's favourite flower. She … she always says their colour is the same as Polly's eyes." He swallowed. "And 'Kettles and pans' is a line from her favourite nursery rhyme – *Oranges and Lemons.* They're the answers to the questions I asked them to put to her so we could be sure she was still alive."

"We've done our bit," said the quietly spoken man. "Now it's your turn. Groby said you're to be our man on the inside at the Naval Board. We need information, details…"

John swallowed again, hard. "The King…" He hesitated, clearly struggling with what to say. Each word could be seen as treason if they weren't able to stop Groby's plot. "The King will be visiting the Navy Board on Seething Lane tomorrow. He will travel from the Tower and is almost certain to approach the office from Crutched Friars. I know all the roads around the Navy Board well, and … I know a spot on that route where

he will be at his most vulnerable. It will, I'm certain, be the only place you'll be able to have a chance at your … scheme."

"Surely with the fire his plans will be changed?" the first man said warily.

"It's a trap!" interjected the less patient accomplice. "The boy is trying to lead us to our capture! We should deal with that pathetic girl now, find some other way to get to the King—"

"No," said John desperately. "Please! The King will come. His Majesty will be determined to show the people that the fire hasn't beaten us, that life will still go on. I know that from my … from my work in his service." His voice wavered, choking on the anguish of giving up more information about the King. "I … I would have been told if the meeting was cancelled, as I'm expected to attend in my role as a clerk. If it wasn't going ahead due to the fire, we would have been told."

"So the offices themselves are unaffected by the fire?" said the first man said.

"The fire hasn't touched Seething Lane and it won't. They say it's heading away to the west. And," John paused, his shoulders sagging, "because they're sending most of his soldiers to help fight the fire, the King probably won't

have as many guards as normal."

Groby's man looked pleased. "Indeed. So tell us what time then, Turner, and, most importantly, where this precious vulnerable spot will be—"

"No." John eyed both men sternly. "If you'd brought my sister to me now, perhaps I could have done. But as it stands, I will not give you more details now, or what reason do you have to keep her alive?" His voice was steady but Beth could see that his eyes were shining with emotion.

"Why you—!"

The quiet man held up his hand to stop his accomplice. "Fine. Listen carefully. At first light tomorrow you are to go to Stonecutter's Yard, off Crutched Friars. You will provide us with the *exact* information we need – *and* stay with us 'til the job is finished."

The more aggressive of the two men stepped closer to John, and in the feeble candlelight from the room Beth could see his flattened nose and an old scar over one eye.

"If you're telling us the truth, you get the girl back then. If anything goes wrong, word will be sent to our boss and you can say 'bye-bye' to your sister."

He turned on his heel and walked away, the other quickly following.

"I hope you know what you're doing, giving them all that information," Beth said, raising a worried eyebrow.

John closed the door and leaned with his back against it, letting out a long breath. "At least I managed to hold them off a bit for now, buy us some more time. And Polly's alive. She's all right – for now..."

But Beth was already easing him out of the way and opening the door, peering down the street. "Forget about waiting until tomorrow. Let's follow them. With any luck, they might lead us to Polly!"

Chapter Eleven

Firefighters

The three spies slipped out of John's house just as the two kidnappers rounded the corner away from Bloodbone Alley. Beth took the lead, and stopped at the corner, cautiously craning her head round.

"They're heading into the city..."

"Come on, then. Let's get after them!" said John impatiently.

But Beth held out a hand. "Wait. Let them get a bit further or they'll hear our footsteps."

A few seconds later, she beckoned them on. At the far end of the street they saw the two men silhouetted in the

glow of the distant fire as they hurriedly walked away. This area was relatively safe from the threat of flames, and there was hardly anyone about at this hour, so Beth knew they would stand out if spotted. They had to be careful. She remembered it was standard spycraft to send someone ahead of the targets, someone who could allow themselves to be overtaken if necessary. Then they would be on hand if those behind lost track of the quarry. But that was impossible now, because the men must have got at least a glimpse of Beth and Ralph while they were standing behind John – they'd be recognized.

"Ralph, you go to the other side of the street and keep ahead of us, but still well back from the men," she whispered quickly. "It's better if we split up. If we lose touch with one another, we'll rendezvous at St Paul's."

Ralph nodded, and darted across the road, quickening his pace 'til he was much closer to the men but still lurking in the shadows of the overhanging roofs above. Before long, the kidnappers came to a crossroads and stopped. The fire was closer now, and they seemed to be discussing the best way to proceed. Beth saw Ralph dodge into a shop doorway. The men started to look around, but she and John had nowhere to go. They flattened themselves against the wall, and Beth prayed

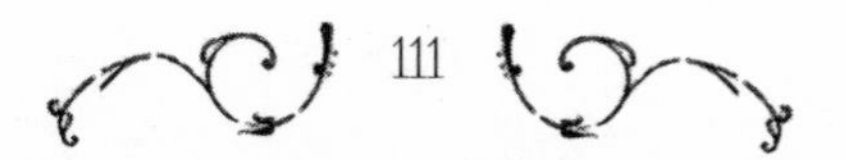

the darkness would hide them. She could hear her own heart drumming as one of them seemed to fix his gaze in their direction. But then his accomplice, the bigger man with the broken nose, pointed down the street to their left and they headed off. Beth saw Ralph slip from his hiding place and scurry after them.

However, the closer they got to the fire, the streets rapidly became more crowded with onlookers and fleeing home owners. Now, being spotted was no longer a worry – it was a matter of keeping the men's heads in view as they bobbed through the throng.

"Good old Ralph," Beth murmured to John. They could see he had taken the initiative and, realizing he could get almost within touching distance with so many people about, he'd closed the gap to within a few yards of the targets.

But then their trail was interrupted. They were skirting the fire at Threadneedle Street, and flames blocked many of the roads here. The crowds were thicker than ever. Beth was still desperately trying to keep her eye on the two men when she was distracted by a panic-stricken cry. A finely dressed but dishevelled man with his wig on sideways, half covering his face, was running around waving his arms about and shrieking at people randomly.

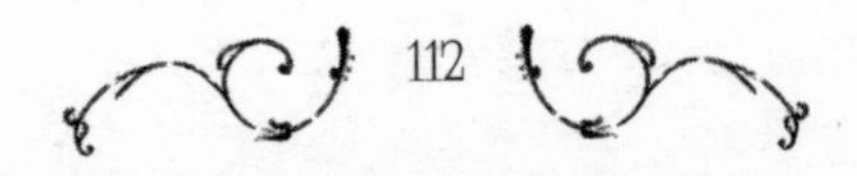

"Lord! What am I to do? I need more soldiers – I need more citizens!"

His eyes fell on Beth and John.

"You there! Please, take poles and set to work! Help us!"

The man picked up some long poles with hooks on the end, like giant shepherds' crooks, and marched towards them just as Ralph came skidding to a halt beside them.

"Where have you been? I lost them in the crowd—!" he hissed.

"Here, you as well," said the man with the poles. "Help us pull the house down at the end of the street before the fire reaches it."

"What? But—" Ralph protested. Beth looked at him, then back into the throng of people. There was no way they'd find the henchmen in this mêlée.

"Just a moment, not the girl!" cried the bewigged man who, despite his panic-stricken state, was evidently in charge. He seemed on the verge of tears and his face glistened red dripped with sweat. "A girl can't handle a pole! Put her with the women carrying water!"

Irritated now, Beth thrust her hands onto her hips and started to march towards him. Perhaps he would like his stupid wig to be thrown into the flames…

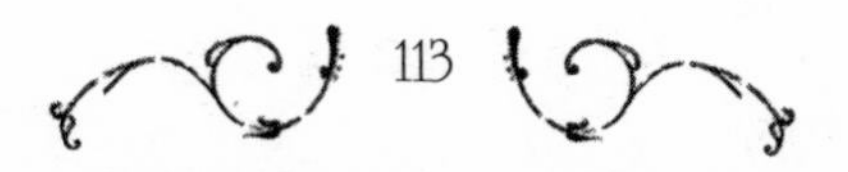

"Easy there, Mistress Beth," Ralph whispered, pulling her back. "You do know who that is, don't you?"

"No, and I don't care!"

"It's the Lord Mayor of London!"

Beth hesitated, and then came to a stop. She knew she ought to respect his authority, even if he was being exceedingly unfair about her abilities. She took a deep breath, muttering under her breath, "Hmm, the very same who thought a young man relieving himself could put this raging fire out? Not so true now, is it?"

Just then a blazing house came crashing to the ground. Sparks and burning debris shot into the air as if from an explosion, and were carried on the wind to the roofs of other buildings. Behind the Lord Mayor was an arc of fire that stretched from one side of London to the other.

"I *could* take a bucket and join the women if you wish, sir," Beth said to the Mayor through clenched teeth. She noticed that the girls and women forming a human chain from the well on Throgmorton Street looked utterly exhausted. She went over to an elderly woman who was visibly sagging, wiping her brow with a bony arm. "Let me," Beth said, taking the leather bucket from her hands. "You are in need of rest."

The woman was too weary to argue, and slumped

down by the side of the road. "Thank you, my dear."

John and Ralph were being told where to go by one of the mayor's officers.

"B-but we're on our way to—" John began to protest.

"No 'buts'!" growled the man. "In case you hadn't noticed, lad, London's burning!"

Looking over the rooftops, Beth estimated that the fire was little more than two streets away and heading in their direction. Her face was roasting, and it was impossible to avoid breathing in the drifting, stinking smoke. She and the other water-carriers continually rubbed their eyes, coughing and spluttering as they worked. It all seemed hopeless. Even a full pail could only contain so much water. No matter how quickly they kept coming, it was hard to believe their efforts could make much impression on an inferno as great as this.

And meanwhile they'd been utterly sidetracked from their mission to find the kidnappers…

Still, the efforts of the men with the fire poles looked more promising. One untouched house had already been pulled down, and now they were working on its neighbour, hoping to create a gap too wide for the fire to leap across. John and Ralph joined forces with some others to set to work on its wood and plaster walls, while

others hacked at the footings with axes. Soon, the whole front of the building toppled forward into the street, creaking like a felled oak. They hopped back as it crashed to the ground, and Beth jumped at the sound. At least if they'd been distracted on their mission to stop Groby's men, they'd been of some help in stopping this dreadful disaster befalling her beloved city…

Chapter Twelve

Moorfields

After finally being released from their duties by the Lord Mayor, Beth, John and Ralph hurried away along the Poultry – the street leading into Cheapside and on to St Paul's. They were discussing their unexpected interlude, and trying to decide what to do next, when a passing man with wild eyes brushed past Beth.

"'Tis the year of the Great Beast. *That* is what all this is about, and now the proof is here…" he shouted as he passed.

"What?" she said to him, both puzzled and alarmed.

"The year 1666 contains within it the sign of the

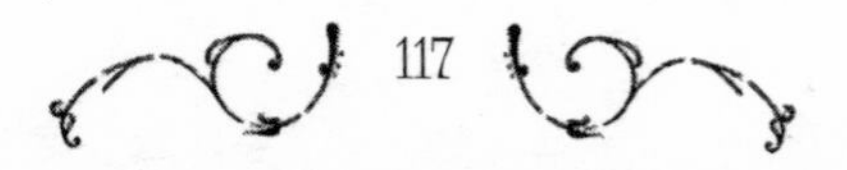

Beast. Six, six, six. *Revelations*, chapter thirteen! Doest thee not know thy Bible, child?"

"But what proof do you speak of?" Beth demanded.

Ignoring her, he passed on, muttering a prayer under his breath.

When they turned the corner, a terrible sight met their eyes and Beth finally knew what the old man meant.

St Paul's Cathedral was ablaze.

Even amid the ghastly scenes of the last two days, this was a shocking sight. Beth, John and Ralph were stopped in their tracks, joining the crowd of silent onlookers. Beth's heart sank. It was like being at a funeral, as if the fate of London had been sealed. If old St Paul's couldn't stand against the fire, then surely nothing could stop it?

"*I knew it...*" John muttered, close to tears.

"What?" Ralph asked.

"St Paul's is gone, with not so much as a signal from Strange before it burned to ashes ... My sister's life is clearly nothing to him."

"But John, Mister Strange himself may be caught up in the fire."

Beth wanted to say more to reassure him, but decided now was not the time to say any more.

John shook his head and ran his fingers through

his hair anxiously. "Ralph, which direction were those men headed?"

Ralph glanced at Beth. "Uh, I actually overheard them saying they were heading to Moorfields – I think those two might have been camped out with the refugees from the city who Beth's theatre mates mentioned…"

John nodded, determined now. "We're going there. We need to find them—"

"Hang on," Beth said, holding up a hand to try and stop John. "I know I suggested we follow them, but seeing as we lost them, it might be too difficult now. We already have a lead on the gang at Somerset House. There's every possibility Polly's there, and I think that's the place we should check first."

"No!" John exclaimed, almost shouting. "We're closer to Moorfields, and to those two bribing thugs. Seeing as Strange isn't around to give us a plan, and it's *my* sister whose life is at stake, I'm going to call the shots. I say we go there."

Ralph sighed. "Listen, mate, I know you're feeling the strain a bit, but we've got a duty to the King as well, so—"

"Duty!" John exploded, stepping towards Ralph. "My poor helpless sister could be killed, and you—"

"Stop it!" Beth said, stepping between the two of them. John's face was red, and not just through anger. She could tell he was embarrassed at his outburst too, and she really did feel for him. Beth felt bad that they might not be doing all they could to find Polly, and time really was of the essence. If they could head Groby's gang off and rescue her sooner, they could prevent the conspiracy against the King altogether.

"John, you must trust that we're here to help. Let's check Moorfields as quickly as we can, and if we can't get a scent of those two thugs, we'll move on. Agreed?"

"Agreed," John said grudgingly, and Ralph nodded too.

Finally they pressed on towards Moorfields and the camp on the outskirts of the city, and as they hurried towards it, Beth tried to push down the worries about what may have happened to Strange. John was right – they were feeling their way through these decisions without his guidance, and the tension was beginning to show…

When they finally arrived, it was the sound of crying that hit Beth harder than anything else. Worse than the shouts of people fleeing the fire, worse than the sound of ravenous flames engulfing the city and the parched

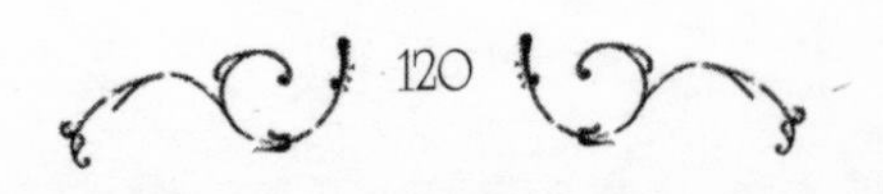

wood of buildings buckling and crashing to the ground. The wailing of babies and uncomprehending young children uprooted from their homes and pursued by the nightmare blaze hit Beth the hardest.

A great sea of humanity filled streets and lanes leading to fields north of London where only a year previously mass graves had been dug for plague victims. The cries of people searching for loved ones from whom they'd become parted filled the night air. Moorfields itself was dotted with tents and makeshift shacks made from pieces of timber, tarpaulin and any other handy materials.

"Lord," Ralph said quietly, "you'd think we were in the camp of a defeated army."

Beth noticed someone wandering among the crowds with a tray of bread held by a strap around his neck. It was only when the smell met her nostrils that she realized she couldn't remember the last time she had had a proper meal.

Ralph was obviously thinking the same. He delved into a pocket and fished out a penny. "We'll take a loaf, friend. Got any cheese?"

The man looked down his nose at the coin without taking it. "Bread's tuppence."

"Doubling your prices just because everybody's

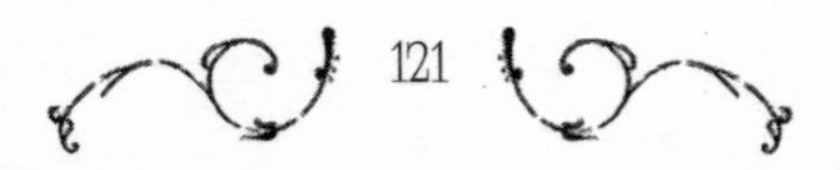

desperate, you villain?" Ralph sneered.

"Take it or leave it."

John found a penny of his own and slapped it on top of the one in Ralph's palm. "Just buy it and let's get on with searching."

Ralph grudgingly handed the money over. "Forget the cheese – and we'll all remember people like you when things are back to normal."

He roughly broke the loaf into three equal pieces, handing one to John and one to Beth as they walked. She took hers and began to gnaw on it eagerly, even snatching up any crumbs that fell onto the front of her dress.

"I feel hungrier now than I did before," Ralph complained when his was gone. His stomach burbled like a blocked drain.

"Me too," said Beth. "But we need to make a start … Hang on – where's John?"

"There!" said Ralph, pointing at a lonely figure wandering from tent to tent, still nibbling at his bread while seeking news of his sister. They went to join him, but he was becoming more and more frantic.

"Wait for us, John!" Beth called. "We ought to do this methodically…"

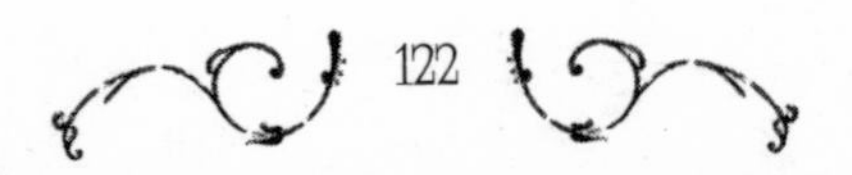

But emotions and desperation seemed to have taken a grip and John suddenly broke into a run, zigzagging between the makeshift shelters. "POLLY! POLLY, WHERE ARE YOU?"

"He's going to let the whole world know about us!" Ralph hissed, running after him.

"POLLY!" John continued, peering into tents and startling families. He sped up a small, sloping hill, calling out desperately and grabbing a young girl by the shoulders who had been walking with a crutch. "Polly? Oh. Sorry … sorry, I thought you were…" He let her go and continued on. "POLLY? WHERE ARE YOU?"

"Stop him!" Beth hissed, heading quickly after Ralph.

"I'm trying. What's he thinking!" Ralph panted angrily.

"John! Stop!" Beth called. Her heart ached for him, but he was completely forgetting all the training they'd had as spies – not to draw attention to themselves unnecessarily.

They raced after John, but his cries and searching was growing even more frantic, and just as Ralph and Beth finally caught up to him, she heard a sneering voice behind her, and whirled round.

It was the two men who had delivered the message,

and the one with the broken nose was laughing at her.

"Your friend's made quite the commotion. Following us, eh? Won't do you any good, darling. The girl's in safe hands – and nowhere near here."

"This was not a clever idea of yours," said the quieter one. He reached into his coat and whipped out a large cudgel, and the other did the same, and they began to advance, swinging out hard at Beth.

"Oi!" Ralph shouted, and John finally stopped and spun around.

"Beth!" John cried, seeing what was happening. He rushed back towards them, and Beth darted out of the way of the man's swipe just in time. John sped down the slope, the momentum giving him extra power as he barrelled the man with the cudgel out of the way, but the other viciously set about him, raining blows down.

Beth sprang into the mêlée, getting between John and the men and trying to block some of the blows with her arms, while Ralph snuck around and caught the coat-tails of one of the attackers, struggling to pull him backwards.

But now three more armed men ran out of the tent the two kidnappers had been standing beside. Beth felt a vicious blow to her forearm that sent a shock running up to her shoulder, the pain so intense that she screamed and fell to the ground clutching her injured arm. John caught a blow to the head with a heavy stick and staggered forwards, tumbling on top of her. Looking beyond him as she struggled to get back to her feet, Beth saw Ralph being lifted off the ground by a tall, powerfully built man. John was dazed and groaning, and Beth fell back to the hard ground under his weight, the pain from her damaged arm still echoing throughout her body.

They were outnumbered.

"Don't leave any traces behind," Beth heard one of their attackers growl.

She was lying on her side in the darkness of the tent. Her hands were tied so tightly behind her back that the pain partly masked that of her throbbing right arm. She twisted her head so she could secretly watch as the villains gathered everything up from inside the tent. Through the open flap she could see them outside, loading a cart with a shabby pony hooked up to it; the pony was pawing the ground impatiently. Turning the other way, Ralph and John came into her vision. Ralph lay with his back to

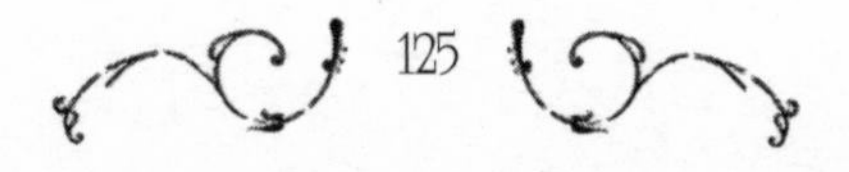

her, but John was in a sitting position, his head lolling forwards. Every now and then he mumbled incoherently, still suffering from the effects of being knocked out.

When the tent was almost empty of belongings, a worrying thought crossed Beth's mind. She, John and Ralph had all got a good look at the men who were working for Groby. What was more important to the villains – getting away as fast as they could, or making sure there were no witnesses left alive whose testimony might one day send them to the gallows? One man came back and picked up the last item, a bulging sack, then went outside and threw it onto the cart. Then a bigger man came back in. Beth half closed her eyes, pretending to be only semi-conscious but leaving just enough of a gap to be able to watch him. He wiped his forehead with his sleeve, and surveyed the insides of the tent. Then a big hairy paw reached for something in his belt that was covered by his loosely flapping shirt. She noticed crude tattoos on his forearms.

He pulled out a long-bladed knife.

Beth squeezed her eyes shut now as he crouched over her, raising the knife in the air. She stifled a gasp, and in the same instant he brought the blade slashing down in a blur. It thudded deep into the hard-baked

ground beside her.

"Don't want that thing sticking in me leg when I'm bending down, do we, girl?" he chuckled. He squatted down, checked the rope round her wrists and tightened it a little, then straightened up with a satisfied grunt and lumbered outside. "You lot better hope you can get out of this little predicament before Groby's expecting ya! Serves ya right." He spat on the ground next to her as he straightened up, pulling the knife out of the ground and tucking it back into his waistband.

The last thing Beth saw of the gang was the men stalking quickly away from the tent, before the canvas flapped shut.

Chapter Thirteen

Captives

"You're the one who always comes up with a plan," Ralph groaned to Beth through the gloom of the tent, trying to get himself into a comfortable position with his bound hands and wrists. "Now would be a good time."

"Well, obviously we need to free ourselves before we can do anything," Beth replied. "I've been working at my ropes but they've done a good job. I'm not making any headway."

"Polly…?" John was finally coming to his senses and was looking frantically around for a sign of his sister.

"I'm sorry, John – she wasn't here, and the gang have

gone," Beth told him quietly.

He began to squirm and struggle at his bindings. "We've got to get out of here…"

"You don't say! Maybe we wouldn't be in this mess if you hadn't gone off yelling—" Ralph began, but a stern look from Beth silenced him.

"You're right," John sighed. "It's my fault. And now we're losing time."

"It's all right," Beth said determinedly. "We'll get out of here." She tried again, but her ropes weren't getting any looser.

"They knew what they were doing," said Ralph. "I know knots from my sailing days, and the way they tied us they'll only get tighter the more you try to pull 'em apart. Let's start shouting."

They began to yell for help, but their voices merely mingled in with the background crackle and roar of the distant fire and the babble of anguished voices all over Moorfields.

Ralph sank back dejectedly. "This is useless."

"No, it's not," John insisted. "People always help each other in a crisis – someone's bound to come eventually."

But John's words had given Beth an idea. "Maybe there *is* something we can do. There was an old preacher

who used to come to St Giles's Church near the Peacock and Pie…"

Ralph groaned. "God isn't going to send an angel down to untie us, no matter how hard we pray."

"No, it's nothing like that. This preacher used to bore everyone to death, but there was one story he told I've always remembered. A man died and ended up in Hell, but there were no flames, no tortures or people in agony. However, everyone was very thin and racked with hunger, even though there was a table laden with every type of food you could imagine. Then he discovered the catch. The Devil only allowed them to eat with a fork about five foot long…"

"So long you couldn't put any food in your mouth," John interjected. "But what good is that to us?"

"I haven't finished!"

"Get on with it, then!" Ralph said impatiently.

Beth sighed and carried on quickly. "God realizes he's made a mistake. The man should have gone to Heaven, so he sends for him. When he gets there, he's puzzled because it looks exactly like Hell, even down to the five-foot forks."

"I hope this is leading somewhere useful," Ralph muttered.

"But the people in Heaven weren't starving – they were well fed and happy!"

"The angels flew down and fed them?"

"Enough of your angels!" Beth chided him.

"Go on, then. Tell me what he did – and *please* make it something to do with untying knots in a tent."

"Simple. The type of people who went to Hell starved because they could only think of feeding themselves. Those in Heaven simply used the long forks to feed each other!"

Ralph's face lit up. "We try to crawl over and untie each other!"

"Bless you, my child," Beth grinned.

"But my legs have gone numb and I can barely move my hands. I'm not even sure if I'd even be able to undo *any* knots."

"I think I can shuffle over to you," Beth said, beginning to kick against the dried-up, yellowing grass. "But you know knots better than I do, so try and get your circulation going and untie mine first."

Beth's bad arm was beneath her body as she wriggled across the ground like an overweight worm, and every movement set off a stabbing pain. She had been trained by Strange not to let it show when she was hurt, but

even she couldn't help letting out a little yelp every time she moved.

"Beth – are you all right?" asked John.

"She took a nasty whack on her arm," Ralph told him. "If it's broken, you could end up permanently crippling yourself, Beth."

"Stop!" John urged her. "Let me try first."

"I'm nearly there..." she gasped. And with a few more pushes of her heels against the ground she had manoeuvred herself so she was back-to-back with Ralph, their bound hands opposite each other. "Now, get to work, sailor boy."

She could feel him fumbling blindly and muttering curses under his breath as he tried to manipulate the rope. It was tied so tightly that even if his hands had been free it would have been hard to prise the strands apart. After a few minutes he stopped and let himself roll away a little, breathing heavily.

"Gettin' cramp in me fingers..."

"Please, Ralph!" John implored.

"He's doing his best," Beth reassured him. "It's harder than it looks."

Ralph took up position again. She felt his nails digging into her wrists as he poked and prodded for an opening,

grunting with the effort. Finally Beth felt something give, and her bindings seemed just a little slacker. Within seconds the pressure had loosened. The blood came surging back into her hands, and they tingled painfully. But that didn't matter – she was free. With spirits rising, she rolled herself into a sitting position to tackle Ralph's bindings. But when she shook the remnants of her ropes away, an intense pain shot through her injured arm that made her cry out and crumple back to the ground.

"Beth! Is it broken?" John asked anxiously.

Once the fog of agony had cleared, she cautiously felt along the bone with shaking fingertips. "I can't feel a break … I'm fairly certain it's just a bad bruise," she decided. It took several more minutes and a broken fingernail, but eventually she had released Ralph, who then quickly untied John.

"Now, can we finally get back to Somerset House?" Ralph asked, brushing himself down.

Beth nodded. "Yes. It should still be safe – it's away from the fire and it's built of stone, so we ought to get there as soon as we can."

"St Paul's is built from stone and should have been safe…" John began glumly. However, once he'd had a second to reflect he perked up a little. "But at least those

scum don't *know* we know it's been their base."

"*And* there's still Ed Hewer. I'm sure he's involved in all this somehow, or at least knows something, and I seemed to be gaining his trust." Ralph grinned. "I'll get him talking all right..."

Chapter Fourteen
The Job

The sky was still dark as they headed towards Somerset House. The fire was still on the move, like a dragon consuming everything in its path. The streets thronged with people who had hoped the inferno would stop short of their home, but were now having to grab what they could and flee at the last minute. There were more mobs on the rampage now too, Beth realized, as they came across a house with its door smashed in and people inside throwing things out of the upstairs windows onto the street below. A neighbour, cowering across the street, informed them that it was the home of a Dutch artist.

The attackers had dragged him outside and started to beat him, but fortunately he had managed to escape.

"This is shameful!" Beth said as they pressed on. "God grant that thugs like that are brought to justice once the fire is out."

"What if it's true?" Ralph ventured. "In wartime people do terrible things, so who's to say the Dutch wouldn't start a fire?"

"But it started at the King's baker's, Thomas Farrinor."

"We don't know that for certain," said John. "It started in that area, but we don't know exactly how."

"*Both* stories could be true," said Ralph. "If it did start in Pudding Lane, what better place for a secret agent to set it going? People would readily believe Farrinor had forgotten to put out one of his ovens at night and a spark had started the whole thing."

Beth had no answer to this. "But roaming the streets of London attacking every Frenchman or Dutchman is still wrong. What if you were living in Paris and a fire broke out? How would you feel if a mob wrecked your home and beat you up?"

But this new way of looking it at had made Beth think. She found herself keeping a sharper lookout for genuinely suspicious characters, or signs that this was the

opening move in an invasion by French or Dutch troops. London would certainly be at their mercy. Or what was left of it.

"We can't solve that problem now," John insisted. "But we *can* try to find my sister and stop Groby. Forget a fire – if this all goes ahead, the King's very life is in danger as well as hers. Can we hurry please?"

Beth felt a little guilty. There was so much to think about that sometimes their main mission slipped into the background. She gave his shoulders a squeeze as they hurried on. "We'll find Polly."

Their route took them to the Strand, from where Beth could look towards Drury Lane. It still looked safe and out of reach of the fire, at least for now. There were homeless people in the streets here but they were coming from further east, and none of the people living in this part of London seemed to have thought it necessary to leave their homes. And yet she couldn't help but think of Maisie. At least the distraction of the fire would stop her from worrying too much about her first performance on stage. Beth had almost forgotten how nervous she had been about *The Empire Dies* and her very first serious lead role, but that all seemed so insignificant now. Who knew if the theatre would even still be standing

after all this?

But there was a gang of conspirators trying to kill the King, using an innocent child as a bargaining chip. It was time to get back to being a spymaster's agent.

Somerset House looked strangely serene after all the sights they had witnessed on their travels through London. Apart from the steady stream of refugees, all was still in the darkness of very early morning here.

"I'll pay the cook a visit again," said Beth. "She's bound to be up starting the baking, and she's a good source of information. Do you think you *can* track down Ed Hewer if he's still here, Ralph?"

"I do. But I think *you* ought to stay out of sight, John. Groby's gang have been dealing with you over Polly, so of the three of us you're more likely to be recognized."

John seemed to see the sense in this and nodded reluctantly. Ralph set off to find Ed Hewer, Lord Cumbria's manservant, leaving Beth to show John the spot beneath the staircase where he could lurk in the shadows.

Ralph hadn't gone five paces before he encountered

a man in his nightshirt, holding a candle and with a fierce look on his face. "And who might you be, boy?" the man demanded haughtily. From his tone, Ralph deduced he was a butler. "What is your business in this establishment, creeping around in the darkness?"

It was only now that Ralph realized he hadn't concocted a cover story in advance. That would teach him. He was so good at talking his way out of situations that it sometimes made him cocky, and now here was this tall, snooty head servant looking down his nose at him, ready to throw him out.

"I'm, er, with Lord Coddingham…"

"There is no gentleman of that title in Somerset House."

"That's true, sir. But on account of the fire and everything he might have to come here, he sent me on ahead."

"Is he acquainted with anyone here?"

Now they were getting into dangerous territory. If he named anyone who was supposed to know an Earl of Coddingham it could be easily checked and his story would fall apart – but his rescue came from an unexpected source.

"It's all right, Mister Warren." It was Hewer. He was

coming up the stairs towards them, and Ralph had never been so relieved to see someone so nefarious before. "This is a cousin of mine," Hewer continued. "He's been hard at work fighting the fire and I asked him to come and let me know he was safe as soon as he could. I've been unable to sleep until I had word of my family."

The butler's brow furrowed for a moment as he gazed from Hewer to Ralph and back again. "It's too late at night for all this to-ing and fro-ing … but the fire is a worry. Still, as all is well now, see that you get to bed forthwith." Then he gave a haughty sniff and strode away.

"Come on," Hewer beckoned. "I'm up early sorting out my master's clothes in his dressing chamber upstairs. Lord Cumbria's the only one left here. Most people think Somerset House is safe – which is why so many of us are still here – but the rest of the gentry are in a panic anyway and leaving for their houses in the country."

"All right for some…"

"Too right. So, what really brings you here, *cousin*?"

Ralph gave him a crooked smile. "Looking to make up me losses."

"What do you mean?"

"Put a bit too much money on a bird that let me down in a cock fight in the back room of the Duke's

Arms. Well, a *lot* too much to tell the truth. One or two people is after me that you *really* don't want to be in debt to…"

Hewer pulled a face. "Look, friend, I'm not that flushed myself 'til I get paid for the special job I told you about."

"Well, I wondered whether you might need an extra pair of hands. You'd take the money you were promised, obviously – just give me a bit of pocket money, like."

Ed Hewer stared at Ralph for so long it began to make him feel uncomfortable. Had he seen through his story? Was he deciding whether or not to alert Groby's men? He mentally plotted his route past Hewer towards the door, ready to run for it if he had to.

But it proved unnecessary. A complete change of mood had come over Hewer. He lowered his voice. "Things have changed. There's a bigger job with a lot more money – but it involves more than just keeping a room free for certain gentlemen. A lot more."

He was uneasy now. Not, Ralph felt sure, just because he was letting someone in on his secret. He seemed to be troubled by whatever it was he was supposed to do for the gang. For a crook like Hewer to be having qualms, it had to be something pretty big.

"As long as it pays well I'll give you a hand whatever it is, matey."

"That's just it … 'tis not a hand I'm looking for. I can't *do* it, Yates. I just can't. But I've a good idea what'll happen to me if I try to back out. I know too much, see."

"So you want to know if *I'll* do it?"

Hewer nodded.

Ralph pretended to think about it, but he was always going to agree. Whatever the job was, he needed to know about it.

"How much?"

"Fifty pounds."

"*Fifty quid?* That's more than both of us could earn in a lifetime! I'm in!"

Hewer had turned pale, and Ralph noticed his hands were shaking. "Don't agree to it 'til you know what it is. I made that mistake."

"Mistake? Look, you'll have to tell me what sort of job we're talking about. But believe me, I've been involved in some serious work in my time. *Very* serious, if you know what I mean."

The most serious thing Ralph had ever done was pick pockets, but he felt sure he sounded pretty convincing.

Hewer took a deep breath. "You'd need to be prepared

to take care of someone…"

"Sure!"

"Permanently."

Ralph knew not to hesitate. "Easy – 'specially if they deserve it!"

"That's just the thing. They don't. Or at least, I can't see how she possibly could. You see, it's a girl. Just a little girl."

Ralph felt a catch in his throat but quickly swallowed it back. "For that kind of money, it's not a problem. She's nobody to me. I'll do it."

Hewer hesitated for a moment longer, and then extended his right hand. "Once we shake on it, there's no going back. I'll take ten per cent for putting the job your way, you keep the rest. But with these people your life will be worth nothing if it isn't done."

Ralph took Hewer's hand and gripped it firmly. He only hoped Hewer hadn't noticed how cold his own hand had become.

"Some of this gang are going into London to carry out a bit of business of their own. If anything goes wrong, word will come back to us and the girl gets it – but if you ask me, knowing the sort of men they are, they'll probably want her dead anyway." Hewer shuddered.

"Meet me here tomorrow, and I'll take you to where the job is to be done."

"All right, matey. Or, if you just tell me where to go I'll make me own way and meet you there…?" Ralph said, hoping Hewer would take the bait.

It didn't work. "More than my life's worth. I've already taken a risk just involving you. Just be here," Hewer said firmly.

Ralph nodded grimly.

He was sure he had just signed up to murder John's sister.

Beth managed to slip downstairs to the kitchen without being seen, and when she got there it was noticeably quieter than before, given the early hour. The cook had her back to her, and there were just a couple of other servants working with her at this time. Beth remembered her cockney orange-seller character at the last moment.

"Er, 'allo there, missus!"

The woman turned from the sink, wiping her hands on her apron, and didn't seem surprised to see her – Beth guessed the cook was used to being up at all hours and

didn't find it odd if others were too. "Why, it's you again. It's Mrs Barnsbury, by the way."

Beth didn't want to give her own name, and the only thing that came to mind was that of her good friend at the Peacock and Pie. "Thank you, Mrs Barnsbury. Uh, I'm Maisie."

"No fruit left?"

Beth grinned. "A lot o' hungry, thirsty people fightin' the fire out there. Got rid of the lot in half an hour, and no more to be had for love nor money."

"There isn't a great deal of food left in here now either, but luckily there aren't many mouths to feed. I'm just about to start the bread." She sighed. "We've had news of all the houses being pulled down or blown up, and everyone says the fire won't reach us, but most of 'em have gone anyway."

"Typical," tutted Beth. "Still a few left, though?"

"Just Lord Cumbria and his two sons. Moved themselves into the rooms the King's mother used to occupy – comfiest bit of the place by far."

"All right for some. Just them, in a big place like this?"

"Well, supposedly..."

Beth didn't want to make it obvious she was after information. She sensed the cook wanted to get it off her chest anyway, so she left Mrs Barnsbury's words hanging in the air and simply arched an eyebrow enquiringly. It worked.

"Young Jenny there," she nodded towards one of her skivvies scrubbing pans, "thinks there's some strange people coming and going in the east wing. But me, I reckon there's something *peculiar* going on."

Beth tensed. Did she know anything about Groby and his men? "Peculiar?" she asked.

"The east wing is where Cromwell's body was taken before his funeral. There's always been tales of strange happenings in this place, and if you ask me he still walks the corridors at night…"

"'Tis real, solid people I've seen," Jenny chipped in, having heard the conversation. "I've seen people moving about through the windows."

"They might look solid from a distance…" the cook said ominously.

"Well, if it's Cromwell, he's wearing noisy boots for a ghost – and carrying a candle at night," Jenny said adamantly.

"Who's to say you can't hear a phantom's footsteps, or see one carrying a candle? Just how much do you know about what phantoms can and can't do, eh?"

"I've always wanted to see a spirit!" Beth said, playing down her interest in the possibility of real humans. "What did they look like, Jenny?"

The girl was scrubbing energetically at a stubborn stain inside a pan as she carried on the conversation. "Hard to tell. They were just sort of flitting past the windows late at night."

"There!" cried Mrs Barnsbury. "Hard to tell because they weren't solid! Cromwell and his anti-royal phantoms won't rest while there's a King on the throne."

Beth felt sure there *was* a presence in Somerset House that wanted to bring down the King – but she was also certain that Jenny's more human explanation was the right one.

Chapter Fifteen

Cromwell's Revenge

"So what did you find out?" asked John urgently. The trio had met up again in the secluded area under the staircase in the grand entrance hall. Through the windows they could see the distant flames and wide curtain of dirty black smoke billowing high into the otherwise clear but dark early-morning sky.

"I found Hewer. Seems I'm getting somewhere with him," said Ralph. "He trusts me and he's telling me things. In fact, he's let me in on a big job they've got on tomorrow."

"It *must* be something to do with Polly," John said.

"What do they want you to do?"

"Er … he didn't go into detail, but I think you're right – probably to do with Polly."

Ralph looked away as John's eyes lit up hopefully.

"That links in with what I found out," said Beth. "The cook thinks the east wing is haunted, but from what we know now, it has to be Groby and his men."

"According to Hewer they'll be back this morning. That's when I've got to do … whatever it is they've got lined up for me."

"So," said Beth thinking out loud, "they're planning to kill the King with our help at the Navy Board, then come back here and release Polly once the job's done."

"Hopefully," said Ralph under his breath.

"What if we can get into the east wing before tonight?" John ventured. "Maybe Polly's in there now – we could get her out then warn the King once she's safe!"

"It's definitely worth a try," said Ralph, glancing at Beth and back to John. "I think I saw the way we'd need to go when I was sneaking about. It was deserted up there."

"The east wing's *supposed* to be deserted, but we must be careful," said John. "We don't know whether or not some of the gang use it to lie low when they're not needed. If we do anything to alert them it might endanger Polly."

"We must be cautious, but I agree we try to get in now," said Beth. "Lead the way, Ralph."

After checking that no one was about, Ralph led them up the left-hand side flight of the two curving staircases that swept up to the next floor. Once at the top they scurried along a corridor. At the end of it, he made them pause.

"Just need to make sure Hewer's not still about," he whispered.

After peering round the corner and listening intently for a few seconds, Ralph set off again, waving them to follow. They came to a left turn leading into another corridor with a large doorway at the end of it, and Beth felt sure the east wing lay behind it. But before they had got halfway down this latest passageway, Ralph stopped again. He turned to John.

"There's nowhere to take cover here if anyone comes. Can you wait at the corner and keep a lookout for us?"

"But you said the place was deserted. I want to be there when – if – we find Polly."

"We can't afford to take any chances…"

Ralph gave Beth the briefest of glances; she knew

it was some sort of signal, and that he wanted her to back him up.

"He's right, John. You can join us as soon as the door's open."

He reluctantly agreed, and sloped back along the corridor to take up station at the corner.

Once he'd gone, Beth and Ralph continued towards the door at the end.

"What's this all about?" Beth asked. "You don't just want him to be a lookout, do you?"

"No," he said in a low voice. "'Tis to do with what Hewer asked me to do." He turned briefly to check that John was out of earshot – but as he did so his shoulder brushed against a bulky plant on a windowsill. It wobbled violently, and was just about to fall when Beth dived forwards and grabbed it before it smashed to the wooden floor.

"Whoops!" said Ralph sheepishly.

"You were saying?" Beth prompted him as she replaced the plant.

"The gang wanted him to do a job. He couldn't, but he daren't refuse them either, so he asked me to do it instead..."

"Do what?"

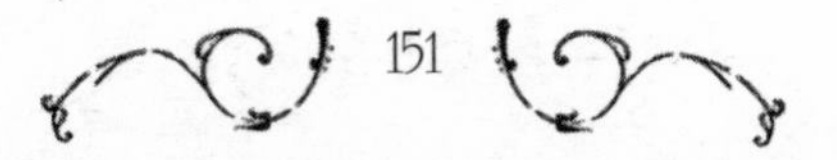

He fixed her with a serious gaze. "Kill Polly."

Beth felt as if an Arctic wind had blown right through her.

"I'm not gonna do it, obviously!"

"I'm relieved to hear it."

"I just thought t'was best if John didn't know. We need him to be on top form, and if you ask me his mood's been a bit dodgy ever since Polly went missing."

"I can't blame him – but you did the right thing. And it's worrying. I know Vale and Groby are ruthless men but I didn't think even they'd go so far as to kill an innocent little girl."

"Well," said Ralph, gently trying the handle of the big door they'd arrived at, "perhaps we can spoil their plan before it's even started. And if we can't, at least I'll be there. Worst comes to worst, you know I'll do my best to rescue young Polly if it comes to it."

"I know you will," Beth said. But she worried that with too many of Groby's thugs around, this might be more difficult than they'd hope. "But let's hope we find her now before it gets to that…"

But Ralph immediately tutted.

"Locked?"

"Yes. All's not lost, though." He pulled his trusty

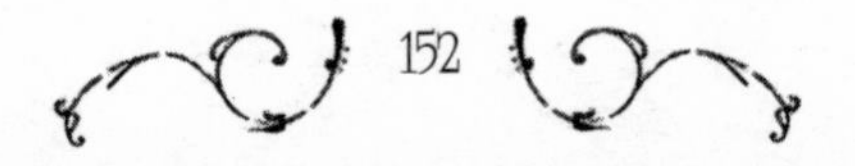

lock-picking kit from the depths of one of his inside pockets and set to work. Within seconds there was a distinct *click*. "Easy! Internal doors are never much of a problem."

But when he pushed at the door, it didn't move. He put his shoulder against it, and still it refused to budge.

"Bolted on the other side?"

"No. They've put something behind it – heavy furniture or something."

Beth gasped. "Does that mean someone's in there? What if they've heard us?"

The waited, but nothing happened. "Well, if they don't react to an unexpected break-in, then they can't be much use. I'd wager they've stacked the furniture against the door but gone out some other way."

They tried the door again, heaving with all their might, but to no avail.

Just then, John came quietly along the corridor. "I think I heard someone coming! Why are you two taking so long?"

Ralph quickly explained the situation to him.

"We have to get out of here, we need to hide," John urged. "Try the door again!"

"It won't open," Beth hissed, glancing up and down

the corridor and trying to listen for footsteps. "I can't hear anything. If Polly's in there, perhaps they've drugged her to keep her quiet…"

"Do we have time to search the house for another entrance?" Ralph hissed.

"John will be due to meet Groby not too long from now … and we might get caught. If someone's moving around up here, it's better we get out of here. And if we can't get this room in the normal way," Beth said, "we'll just have to do it the hard way."

She began hurrying away down the corridor, and Ralph and John followed.

"I'm not sure I like the sound of this," Ralph whispered. "Your plans always seem to end up in some death-defying stunt—"

"The idea I've got might be dirty and uncomfortable, but it should be reasonably safe."

"There, you see. *Reasonably.* Reasonably makes me nervous," he hissed.

"Among your many careers, were you ever a chimney sweep as a young boy?" she asked Ralph.

"You think we can get in down the *chimney*?" John whispered incredulously. "Surely there's another way?"

"We don't have time to start another search," Beth

replied. "It's been a hot summer so they won't have had a fire in ages. And everyone's too busy looking at the London fire to notice us. Why not?"

"If it means saving Polly, I'll walk through walls," John replied.

But Ralph had gone strangely quiet.

"Don't you think it's a good idea?" Beth asked.

"Might be tricky, to say the least. Chimneys tend to be fairly narrow … But if we must, we must."

Ralph didn't seem his usual self now, and she thought perhaps it was what he was supposed to do to Polly. But whatever the problem, there was no time to get to the bottom of it. They slipped quietly out of the house and into the garden at the rear, where they were less likely to be seen in the gloom. To give themselves time to plan their entry, they took refuge behind a large, ornate bush.

Ralph let out a quiet whistle. "That place has got lots of chimneys…"

"Yes," said Beth, "but we're only interested in the east wing, which is on the right of the building. If we can work out roughly where the blocked door was, we can see which chimneys are beyond it."

Ralph scrutinized the building, then suddenly perked up. "That window!" he said, pointing to the top floor.

"There's the plant on the windowsill I nearly sent flying!"

"So that big chimney stack at the corner leads to a fireplace on the other side of the door!" Beth finished for him.

"We need to start at that drainpipe," John decided. After checking that the coast was clear, he led them quickly across the lawn to a metal pipe attached to the pale stone wall. The good thing, Beth thought, was that it was located in a quiet, dark corner: a right-angle where the main building met the east wing.

John was in such a hurry that he had started his ascent before she and Ralph had joined him.

"Careful, matey – looks a bit rusty," Ralph warned.

"It is," came the whisper from above. "But it feels strong enough."

Soon all three of them were shinning up the pipe, with Beth taking up the rear. She could feel the rough patches of rust under her grasp. In places the metal was so corroded her fingers almost went right through and bits of wafer-thin rusty metalwork came away, fluttering to the ground below. She watched them fall, and only now realized how high they already were. Just as she thought it, a whole section of pipe came away in John's hand. He swayed back with a cry of alarm, his legs squeezed against the lower part of the pipe preventing him from falling. Ralph quickly reached up a hand and supported him.

"I can't believe you've got us into this," Ralph muttered.

"What am I supposed to do with this?" John asked, the section of broken piping still in this hand. "If I drop it someone might hear it land, but I can't climb while I'm holding it."

"Put it on that window ledge beside you," Ralph hissed.

"It won't stay on there for long," Beth warned.

"No, but if he jams it in place as best he can it might stay put long enough," Ralph whispered irritably. "There's no other option."

John reached across to his right and put the rusty pipe on top of an upper window ledge. Beth knew a strong gust of wind would soon bring it down, but it was the best they could do. Her hands, arms and legs were burning by the time they resumed their climb, but now there were only a few feet to go.

"I can't get a foothold to climb over the ledge onto the roof," John hissed as they reached the top.

"Use my shoulder," Ralph whispered. "But quickly,

I can't hold on much longer!"

John made an extra effort to get himself onto the roof – but his boot dug deep onto Ralph's shoulder, and one of Ralph's hands slipped free from the pipe. In his haste to regain his grip, Ralph only succeeded in clutching John's leg and yanking hard on it. He stifled a scream as he lost his grasp of the ledge. A sudden image of them both tumbling through space flashed into Beth's mind. She screwed her eyes tightly, letting out a little whimper, but then John's hand caught onto the ledge and he pulled himself up. Once he was up on the roof he reached down to help the others up.

"That was nothing compared to the maintop of a frigate in a gale!" Ralph breezily informed them, brushing off the shock of their near-miss. Now they were on the flat, leaded roof, they could walk along it towards the chimney stack with comparative ease. But the chimney was much taller than it had appeared from the ground. Then Beth realized that, being Somerset House, even the chimney stack had a decorative pattern in the brickwork, and some bricks stuck out to form a sort of spiral pattern running from bottom to top.

"They've even made a sort of staircase for us out of bricks," she said.

"Very thoughtful of them," said Ralph.

But there was a sort of breathlessness to his voice, and Beth noticed he'd suddenly become strangely subdued again.

"Did you hurt yourself?"

"No," he mumbled, looking up at their next challenge. "It's just that chimney..."

"But I thought you were good with heights? You are the sailor boy after all – climbing masts and everything!"

"That's just it. Heights are meat and drink to me – 'tis *depths* sailors don't like. This one, 'specially."

Now Beth thought she understood what had come over him ever since this plan had been raised. "You mean going *down* the chimney? You don't like being closed in?"

He had turned pale and was starting to shake. "Can't stand feeling trapped..."

John was becoming impatient. "It's not that far down. Just close your eyes and get it over with as quickly as you can."

"I'll go first," Beth declared. Perhaps by setting an example she might boost Ralph's confidence.

"No, let me go first and get it over with," he said quickly. But he didn't make a move towards the chimney, and Beth began gathering up her skirts to prepare for

the descent. She noticed John reddening slightly at this, turning his face away from her with an embarrassed cough. But Ralph was still sizing up the chimney like someone facing the hangman's noose. Beth had never seen him so frightened.

"Perhaps I ought to go last?" he now decided. "If I see you two do it all right, it'll make me feel better…"

"Oh, for heaven's sake!" said John, making for the chimney. "My sister's life is at stake!"

"All right, all right' Ralph hissed, suddenly springing in front of him and commencing the climb. "I've changed my mind. I'll go first!"

They all ascended the chimney, using the pattern of bricks that protruded like the sawn-off branches of a monkey puzzle tree. Beth followed Ralph, with John coming up behind. When he got to the top, Ralph hovered at the edge and looked down into the blackness.

"Lord … what if it's too narrow?"

Beth worked her way round to the other side 'til she was at the top with him. "Ralph, we'll easily get down there. It will be a squeeze, yes, but there's no possibility of getting stuck – trust me."

With a deep breath, Ralph swung his legs over 'til he was sitting on the edge of the chimney with his

feet dangling inside.

"Just use your arms and feet against the sides to stop yourself from falling," Beth urged him. "We had a sweep who used to come into the Peacock and Pie, and his boy told me most chimneys aren't completely straight on the inside. There's usually a kink, and plenty of uneven bricks and crevices for foot-holds."

Ralph's breath was coming in short, shaky bursts now. Without looking down, he began to lower himself bit by bit until his head disappeared from view. Beth quickly scrambled over the top so that she would be close behind him, with John queuing behind her, itching to go. Soot dislodged by Ralph wafted upwards on a draught from the fireplace. Beth had to pause, blinking and rubbing her eyes. She could hear Ralph coughing in the darkness below but she could no longer see him – but then finally she heard his whisper, relief flooding into his voice.

"I'm nearly there! I can see the bottom!"

"Carefully," Beth cautioned. They still didn't know what – or who – might greet them once they finally got into the room.

Still, it sounded as if he more or less let himself fall the last few feet, and his landing sent a cloud of black dust billowing into Beth's face.

"All clear," Ralph called, and Beth felt a wash of relief.

Before long, the three of them were sprawled in the hearth of a huge open fireplace. Beth looked around quickly, dusting herself off.

"Polly? Is she here?" came John's anxious voice as they stood up and looked around. But there was nobody at all in the room. Beth's heart sank – she could only imagine John's disappointment.

Ralph was panting and bedraggled, but freed at last from his nightmare he grinned and pointed at John. "Look at you!" he laughed.

John's face was black all but for his blinking white eyes. His brown hair stood on end, and a little cloud of dust hung over him like his own personal rain cloud.

"Look at *you*, you mean!" John retorted. Ralph was in the same shape as John, and Beth, tasting the soot in her mouth, knew she must look just as bad. For a moment they stood recovering their breath, and she surveyed their new surroundings. The room had bare, dark wooden floorboards, a single bookcase, and several old portraits hanging on the walls. But it was a big space and had an abandoned look to it, virtually stripped of furniture as it was apart from a bulky chest of drawers that had been pushed up against the door.

"How on earth did they get out of here after blocking the door? I can't see any other exits," Beth mused, frowning. "Unless they went out the same we just came in? Seems so unlikely, though…"

The others looked around, just as perplexed. The only signs of recent human habitation were in one corner, away from the windows – but they were telling ones.

Blankets were spread out on the floor as if to make temporary beds. There were a couple of little bundles wrapped in large cotton handkerchiefs, and the remains of a meal: a half-eaten pie, some apple cores and two wooden tankards.

"I can't believe Polly's not here," John murmured sadly. He gazed into the corner, as if he might get a glimpse of his sister's presence if he tried only hard enough.

"Well, I'll get Hewer to take me to her. He knows where she is, even if he—" Ralph's voice suddenly faltered.

"What?" John demanded. "What about Hewer?"

"I … I thought t'was best not to tell you…"

"We didn't want to panic you," Beth added.

John's eyes narrowed. "What? That's why you got rid of me when you were checking the door into here, isn't it? You didn't need a lookout – you just wanted to form

a plan between yourselves and keep me out of it."

Beth went over to him and grasped his grimy hand. "We weren't excluding you. We didn't want to burden you with it."

He softened a little. "But why would it be a burden?"

Ralph looked to Beth, and she nodded. John might as well know everything now – it was only fair. "I don't think … well, from what Hewer says, I don't think they intend to let her go."

The terrible truth dawned on John. "They're going to kill her once they've got what they want from us, aren't they?"

"Ed Hewer is in on it, but he couldn't bring himself to do it. So … he asked me."

Beth expected John to explode, so she was surprised by the way he took this news.

"But that's good! You're on the inside now, and you can make sure nothing happens to her!"

Ralph exhaled. "That's the plan. And I'll do everything I can to protect her. But I don't know the details yet. I'm meeting Hewer here later this morning, and he'll take me to wherever she is. I tried to get it out of him earlier, but it was no good, and I couldn't risk making him suspicious. I'm just hoping there's not too many of them to fend off if it comes to it, or whether they'll all be breathing down my neck when the time comes to—"

John jumped to his feet. "But you won't go through with it!"

Ralph quickly shook his head. "Of course not! Rather let 'em kill me than do that, matey!"

John exhaled and gave Ralph a silent nod of gratitude.

"Whatever their plan for Polly is," Beth said, "they're bound to wait 'til you tell them where the King will be most vulnerable on his route to the Navy Board, as you promised. She's their bargaining tool."

John let out a sigh. "Let's clean off a bit – Ralph, you can't turn up to Hewer looking like that or he'll know something is up. Then when we're sure the coast is clear, we can shove that chest of drawers out of the way and slip out through the back door."

They did their best to brush the soot off their clothes and wipe off their faces, giving Ralph some extra help to make him as presentable as they could. Beth could still feel the dust and soot in her hair and nostrils, and every time she swallowed she tasted tiny, bitter granules.

"Very well," she said. "Let's move this furniture away from the door – slowly – and check if the coast is clear…"

They began to move the chest of drawers, inch by inch

so as not to make too much noise, then waited, pressing their ears to the door. But when they heard a sudden creaking noise it wasn't from the corridor – it was from behind them, *inside* the room. The three of them whirled around, staring around them desperately.

"Did you hear that?" John whispered.

"Yes," came Ralph's reply.

"Is there someone in here?"

Beth could see a big oil painting, one she knew had been hanging on the wall next to a large bookcase, resting at a crazy angle on the floor.

"H-how did that portrait come off the wall?" Ralph whispered.

The stern, warty figure in it appeared to be glaring right at them, as if resenting their intrusion. He looked familiar. Beth got onto her hands and knees and crawled a little closer. It was Oliver Cromwell.

"Cook says this wing is where his body lay in state before the funeral," she told them. "I'm amazed they didn't find this and take it down when the royals took over the residence again."

"Whose body?" Ralph asked.

She gestured to the painting. "Cromwell. She reckoned he haunts the place."

"Well, I don't believe in ghosts," John said quickly.

Ralph shook his head. "I always thought there was something spooky about this place. I was on the dockside in Wapping one night, when out of the corner of my eye I saw—"

"Wait!" Beth shushed him. She had seen a movement on the upper shelf of the bookcase on the far side of the room.

"Mouse?" John ventured.

There was a scraping, scratching sound. The whole bookcase seemed to tremble, and one of the books seemed to twitch, at first almost imperceptibly, then more violently.

"Bloomin' strong mouse," Ralph muttered.

The book gave one extra strong shudder, then suddenly fell from the shelf, its pages flapping open. Beth's skin was crawling as if a thousand spiders were rushing over her. As a spy she was used to preparing herself to meet a threat, but somehow this felt different. Summoning all her courage, she slowly edged towards the dusty volume and picked it up.

"Maybe it is Cromwell's ghost. Maybe he doesn't want us here – we are the King's spies..." Ralph muttered.

"Nonsense!" hissed John, but even he sounded

unsure now.

Beth was sure there was a good explanation, but as with Ralph and his seafaring background, the theatrical world she inhabited was full of superstition. She turned the book over to look at the cover. The room was warm, but the book felt oddly cold. She stared at its title:

Cromwell's Revenge.

Just then the bookcase began to shake and creak. Beth stifled a yell and dashed back towards her friends. When she turned to look back, a shadowy figure had materialized before them, making no sound. All she could hear was Ralph muttering the Lord's Prayer under his breath.

The figure emitted a deep chuckle and stepped away from the bookcase, which had moved away from the wall at an angle, leaving a dark gap on one side.

"Certain people have far more reason to be afraid of me than of Cromwell's ghost…"

He continued to advance, and now they could see his face.

It was Sir Alan Strange.

Chapter Sixteen

Blackfriars

"It seems that you haven't learned that Sir Henry Vale is also back in England, controlling Groby and his henchmen," said Strange. They were all standing in a circle, close to the secret hiding place behind the bookcase from which their spymaster had emerged. He'd explained that there were often networks of secret passageways in buildings like this, and he'd followed some intelligence about the plot against the King which had led him there. Beth was relieved they had a way to sneak out of there, at least…

Strange had listened as they quickly filled him in on

how they'd ended up there, but now Beth, John and Ralph looked at one another, absorbing this information about Vale. It was somewhat inevitable that he was behind all this, Beth thought bitterly. The famed anti-Royalist had been behind all the plots they'd faced down against the King so far, since he'd faked his own beheading several years prior.

"I already had people trying to observe Vale," Strange continued, "but we were unaware of what Groby's part was in his leader's scheme until you alerted me to his activities. As you can imagine, it's been hard conducting good espionage with the fire raging. Several of my people are not contactable, hence my pursuing this lead myself. Vale and his men have been very elusive and hard to keep track of – you must have found out about Somerset House before us."

"It was through a man called Ed Hewer, a servant here," Beth explained. "He's involved with Groby's gang, and Ralph has managed to gain his confidence."

Strange gave a rare, slow smile. "Well done, Ralph. All of you. How is this Hewer connected to Groby, and what is his role in all this?"

"He's not really one of their men," Ralph explained. "It started with them bribing him to let them use this

place as a base – and then they wanted him to do something far worse."

"What thing? Name it."

Ralph was looking sheepishly in John's direction, and it was John himself who intervened.

"Kill my sister. They plan to assassinate the King when he visits the Navy Board in the morning, and will kill her if anything goes wrong. We've tried to—"

"Hold," Strange interrupted sharply. "How do they plan to get close to the King when he visits the Navy Board tomorrow?"

"John had to promise to help them in order to keep Polly alive," Beth admitted. "It was the only option we had."

Strange glowered at the three of them for a moment. "I expect my spies to *obtain* information, not give it to the enemy."

"I … I know, sir," John stuttered. "But I had to do something to hold them off from harming my sister, and our hope is to stop them before they manage to harm the King—"

"And in playing them along," Beth interjected, "we hope to find out where Polly is. If we rescue Polly, we can foil Groby and stop him and the others in

their plot against the King!"

"It is absolutely not acceptable that your information has put the King in more danger." Strange glowered at them, but then his expression softened slightly. "But at least now we know the nature of the threat to His Majesty. I will flood the area with the King's guard and—"

"No!" exclaimed Beth, before lowering her voice. "With all due respect, sir, that will alert them and they'll kill Polly before we have a chance to stop them. Please let us proceed with our plan, John will meet with them tomorrow and we can somehow lay an ambush then, once we know the girl is safe."

"So, where is Polly? How do you plan to ensure her safety while duping Groby?"

Beth's head dropped a little. "We don't know yet…"

"Trust us, Mister Strange!" Ralph pleaded. "I'm meeting Hewer later on – he's going to take me to Polly. And Beth will go with John to meet Groby. Between us, we'll stop them!"

"Have we ever failed you?" John added.

Strange fixed each of their gazes for a moment but did not answer the question. He was silent for what felt to Beth like an agonizing length of time before replying.

"I will allow you to continue," he said. "And there will

be no extra guards for the King to draw attention. But before you do anything rash, you must inform me of your plan once it's formulated. I will be in the guardhouse at the main entrance to the Tower until the King's carriage leaves. And I will station a number of my people whom I *have* been able to contact in ordinary clothes in the area. They are good at their job and Groby won't spot them – but if the King appears to be in *any* danger they will intervene, whether you have rescued Polly or not. Is that understood?"

As they were now were able to use Strange's secret passage, Beth and John were able to slip out of Somerset House this time both quickly and unnoticed. Ralph remained in place, ready to pretend to help Ed Hewer in his gruesome task.

Beth took a deep breath. It felt good to be out in the cool air and stretch her legs after the stuffy, ominous atmosphere of the east wing.

Even in the growing morning light, the still-raging fire was impossible to ignore. It dominated the skyline like a rip in the world exposing a glimpse of Hell. Beth

could feel the warmth on her face, carried over half a mile on the steady breeze from the east. Streets that would normally be deserted at this hour echoed to the sound of rattling cartwheels and shuffling footsteps. More and more people were being forced from their homes. But the closer she and John got to St James's Park near the Palace of Westminster, well away from the fire, they began to encounter fewer and fewer people.

"What's the plan, Beth?" asked John. "We're not far off the meeting place with Groby."

"I thought Captain Jack Turner would be the one to come up with a plan!"

He smiled, but it was a rather sad smile. "If only I really *were* Captain Jack, people might take me more seriously…"

"*People?*" Despite the circumstances, she was being a little mischievous, knowing what he meant to say but was too shy to.

"People who think I'm too shy and timid for this sort of thing. Ralph, Strange … and … and…"

"I can't think what other names you can possibly come up with. I, for example, very much like the quiet John. Just as much as the dashing Captain Jack – more, in fact. *He* would probably wear me out with all his

leaping about and swordfighting."

John laughed a little, but he turned to her as they walked and caught her gaze. "I wish I could believe that."

For a moment it was as if the fire, the kidnappers and the plot against the King didn't exist, and they were simply out for a moonlit stroll together.

"You *should* believe it."

He drew closer to her. "Beth..."

"Yes?"

"When this is all over—"

"*Who goes there?!*"

A man with a pikestaff jumped out at them, and for a second Beth thought they'd been ambushed by Groby's men. But their route to Stonecutter's Yard, where Groby had told John to meet the gang, had taken them close to the Tower of London, and it was one of the uniformed guards on a routine patrol.

"We're on an important assignment for one of the King's most trusted officers," said John without a moment's hesitation.

"Oh, is that right? Sure you wouldn't rather I arrange for you to see His Majesty himself? I'm sure he wouldn't mind if we woke him up."

"Strange," said John quietly.

"You're too right it is," the guard began. He seemed just about to call for assistance.

"Sir *Alan* Strange," John said, lowering his voice. "We are in his … employ. 'Tis not something we can discuss with you – unless you want to answer to him over the matter."

The guard's sneer instantly vanished the moment the feared spymaster's name was mentioned.

"Of course," John continued, "if we're late for our rendezvous, we shall have to explain the cause of it. What did you say your name was?"

The man lowered his formidable pikestaff. "Now, now. There's been no delay, not as matters anyway. So don't you go saying there has. Off you go."

"Nicely done, Captain Jack!" Beth said as they hurried on. "But we still need a firm plan when we get to where you're to meet Groby."

"How about … I'll draw him away from the others and whack him, you take care of whoever's left. If they're all unconscious, they won't be able to get word to their thugs to kill Polly, *or* get to the King."

"That's a plan?"

"It's easy enough in Captain Jack's world."

Beth wasn't sure whether he was joking or not, but it

struck her that it was as good an idea as any. “Well, we’ll have the element of surprise, I suppose. And if we can arm ourselves…”

They were entering Crutched Friars now, and the growing daylight cast the windows and roofs in a warm glow.

“Grab one of these branches,” said John, casting his eye over the churchyard of St Olave’s on the corner of Seething Lane. “And some heavy stones. Anything stout enough to whack someone but small enough to conceal ’til the time’s right.”

“Aye, aye, captain!” said Beth, and quickly grabbing suitable weapons from the ground.

Then they just had to wait.

“Someone’s coming…” whispered Beth. They were in the shadows at the corner of Stonecutter’s Yard, Groby’s meeting place. Footsteps could be heard coming from the direction of Whitechapel. They sank back, and before long Beth saw shadowy figures emerging out of the morning gloom, heading their way.

“Ready?” Beth asked.

"Ready as I'll ever be," John replied.

She took a deep breath, gave his forearm a quick, hard squeeze, and then turned into the yard and hurried to her hiding place behind a tarpaulin-covered cart. There were three men approaching, and from her vantage point Beth could just make out the squat figure of Edmund Groby. The other two hung back, constantly looking around as if hoping to protect their leader from an ambush from either end of Crutched Friars. She could only make out dark outlines, but one was like a taller version of Groby: thick-set, with a short, fat neck and squarish head, and big shoulders filling out his jacket. The other looked older – he might be the weak link when it came to a fight, and Beth felt better about her chances of taking on the two of them now.

It was John she was worried about. Groby on his own would be a handful, even for a skilled and experienced fighter like Strange. All their joking about Captain Jack aside, she knew John *did* possess courage – but it was hard to believe that would be enough against a thug like that. She hastily pushed an image of what might become him at Groby's hands out of her mind…

She heard John saying something about Groby sending his men into the yard while they talked, but Groby had

ideas of his own. Beth couldn't hear everything that was said, but it was Groby himself, accompanied by John, who came into the yard while the other two waited at the entrance. Beth cursed silently to herself as Groby positioned himself by the cart. There was no risk of being seen as she was on the other side of the yard, and in almost total shadow. But her plans to make a surprise attack on the two henchmen were dashed. She could help John with Groby, but the others would be alerted immediately. If they could deal with Groby quickly enough the plan might still work…

Beth decided to wait to hear what he had to say before making her move.

"So, you came after all," she heard Groby sneer in his unpleasant, rasping tone.

"I've kept my promise," replied John. "Now you must keep yours. Release my sister."

Groby laughed. "Ah, well you haven't quite fulfilled your promise yet, have you, young sir? We still need to know the time, and the King's precise route, and most importantly this place where you say we may conceal ourselves when he will be at his most vulnerable."

"Very well. I … I can tell you—"

"I haven't finished," Groby cut in harshly. "Don't

think I've forgotten the little matter of an attempt by certain persons to follow my men to Moorfields?"

"I have no idea what you're talking about," John said flatly. Beth was surprised at what a good liar he could be, but she knew Groby wouldn't be fooled, and she was right.

He laughed again, though it sounded like the harsh cawing of a crow. "Ah, so there are other young people running around London trying to track a young crippled girl down?" His tone became darker. "To be clear – if there are any further such attempts to second guess us, I will order the girl killed on the spot. Now, tell me what I need to know."

John sighed heavily and hesitated, as if having to force himself to answer. Beth held her breath. Would he really tell Groby the truth. She could see he had no choice. They had to do something to stop Groby before he actually got close to the King.

"His Majesty will leave the Tower in his carriage shortly before ten this morning," John began, his voice shaking with the duress. "He will make his way to the Navy Board's office close by here on Seething Lane, to inspect the plans for the new ship, the *Royal Charles*. His … His carriage will go up Tower Hill and into Woodrofe

Lane, which meets Crutched Friars. But about half way up Woodrofe Lane is Draper's Alley. It is a place of decayed houses, boarded up and awaiting demolition, so there will be no one looking on. It is also open at both ends – and at the end opposite to Crutched Friars there is an escape route to Tower Hill and the river. Here..." To prove the truth of what he was saying, John produced his own copy of the itinerary. Beth realized he must have been carrying it with him all this time, in case of just such a crisis point.

Groby took a cursory glance at the document, nodding. "Very well. Even an escape route – you *do* think like a spy!"

Beth's heart quickened. What was to stop Groby just killing John now, as well as Polly?

"Then you will release Polly?" John said hopefully.

"Ah, that would be a little premature, wouldn't it, boy? When the King lies dead and cold, you will be repaid with her freedom. If the deed is not completed successfully, *another* will be found face that fate."

"But—"

"No 'buts', Master Turner. Wait there a moment while I pass your helpful information on to my colleagues."

Groby returned to the other men. There was a brief

conversation, and when he returned, he was followed by the older man.

"It is arranged," Groby growled.

"Good," John said tightly, looking between the men. Beth could tell he was clenching and unclenching his fists, looking for a chance to try and strike out at Groby. She crouched, ready to join him. "I shall await my sister at our house in Bloodbone—"

"Not so fast." The man lurking in the background stepped forward and spoke for the first time. She could see now that he was wearing a fine coat trimmed with lace, and wore a gentleman's dark wig.

Beth had to suppress a gasp. It was Sir Henry Vale.

"Did you think we were going to risk *our* necks, boy?" said Vale, reaching into his coat. "And besides, what's to stop you running off now and tipping off the authorities?" He produced a pistol and held the stock of it out to John, whose face blanched as he too realized who the man was.

"I – I *can't*—"

"Oh, you *can*, Turner. It's just a question of whether you *will*, isn't it?" He forced the flintlock pistol into John's hand and stepped back. "There, now. It's loaded." A slow smile spread on his face. His voice was like velvet.

"You could shoot me dead on the spot should you wish to. You would like to do that, I'll wager. But dear little Polly would then die too, of course. Though you'd never know about that because my friend here would kill you first. So it all comes down to this – whether you value your own life above that of your sister."

Chapter Seventeen

A Plan

As soon as everyone had cleared Stonecutter's Yard, Beth slipped from her hiding place. She had to follow them, try and figure out how to stop Vale's plan.

Stay calm, John, she prayed silently. She just caught sight of the group disappearing out of sight, but she decided it shouldn't be too difficult to find them. She didn't know Draper's Alley, but she knew it must be very close, because Woodrofe Street was just round the corner from where she was. Thanks to what John had said about an escape route at the other end, she also knew that it must be accessible from the next street.

Instead of following, she skirted round to the right where she caught sight of a narrow little lane running parallel with Woodrofe Lane. That had to be Draper's Alley. But just as she was about to cross Crutched Friars, she noticed a red glow in a shop doorway across the road and froze, still hidden in the shadows of the tall buildings behind her.

She realized the red glow was a man's pipe, and she could just see his dark form fidgeting in the doorway. After a few moments, he leaned forwards and looked left and right. Instinct told Beth that he was one of Vale's own spies. Strange's men wouldn't allow themselves to be so easily spotted. If he even *sniffed* that Beth was following his master, or suspected any other moves against Vale and his gang, then he or others like him would slip away and tell the people holding Polly to carry out their misdeed.

All her senses were heightened now. There had to be more than one. She scanned the street, and looking up Poor Jewry Lane she saw two men standing outside a butcher's shop. They were not trying to hide, but seemed to be wearing workman's clothes and just casually chatting as if on their way to the docks or warehouses for an early start. But as Beth watched she noticed that both were actually spending more time glancing up and

down the street than looking at each other.

Beth edged along the wall, stopping every few seconds to check that doorways and windows were clear. Eventually she reached a point where she was as sure as could be that she was out of sight of suspicious eyes. She slipped silently across Crutched Friars at a narrow point and into Draper's Alley. It was just as John said – derelict. People had been using it to abandon their rubbish, and Beth was grateful for this because the old boxes and broken bedsteads made good hiding places. She took a few paces into the alley and dipped down between two wooden crates. She could hear hushed voices, but not what was being said. It would be dangerous to try to get closer, but she had to.

With a racing heart, she crawled from her hiding place on her hands and knees. Just as she was about to hide behind a stinking pile of sacks filled with rotting vegetables, her hand caught a loose potato on the ground and flicked it across the lane. It bounced and bobbled in virtual silence – until it hit a stick and sent it spinning across the ground. The voices at the other end of the alley instantly fell silent.

"Someone's there…"

It was Vale. But Groby, of all people, saved her.

"Nah, I saw it. Just a rat, sir."

Their hushed voices resumed their earlier conversation, and Beth was finally able to breathe again as she hid herself behind the sacks and peered over the top. Vale, Groby and the other man were standing in a circle around John.

"As soon as the King's carriage passes," Vale was saying, "you shall step out, waving. I know you have met the King – and your precious spymaster Strange will probably be with him anyway – so should not cause alarm. You will say the wind has changed direction and is blowing the fire towards the Navy Offices, and you have been sent to tell His Majesty's procession that the meeting has been cancelled and the offices evacuated."

"B-but someone's bound to realize the wind hasn't changed, that the fire is not coming this way..."

"That matters not. By this time you will be close to the King. You will reach into your coat ... and I hardly need to tell you what to do next," Vale sneered.

Beth had been taught that plans rarely worked out exactly as expected, and the true test of a spy was how to think on your feet when the unexpected happened. Avoiding attracting any attention this time, she crept silently out of Draper's Alley. It was time to think on her feet...

* * *

The King didn't normally reside at the Tower; Beth guessed he wanted to be close enough to the fire to help co-ordinate the fight to halt its progress. Security around the perimeter was every bit as strong as Beth would have expected. However, as soon as a special password Strange had given them was mentioned, her path was cleared as if by magic. She was led into the guardhouse, a large barrack-type building just inside the main entrance, and past a number of soldiers putting on helmets and metal breastplates. One caught her eye because he was surprisingly small for any sort of soldier, let alone the King's own guard.

"You don't have to be big to be in the elite guard," said a familiar voice. "Just very, very good." It was Strange. "Isn't that right, Hawkins?"

The soldier saluted, and smiled at Beth. She realized that although he was not much taller than her, like her he had an athletic build. In fact, he had given her an idea … Beth quickly returned his smile and turned to Strange.

"Where is Turner?" he said.

"I've got something to report," Beth said anxiously.

"Let's go where we won't be disturbed…"

* * *

"I see," Strange said once she'd finished. "John finds himself in a most trying position." *To say the least*, Beth thought. They were in a little office at the back of the guardroom. There was a rough sketch of the King's route that morning pinned to the wall, and Beth saw that it had various small "x"s marked on it. She guessed this was where Strange's own men were posted, and realized she must have walked right past one of them without even knowing.

"I hope he will keep his head," Strange continued, "I confess I sometimes wonder about him."

"He will cope. We just need to determine a way to help him."

It came out a little more sharply than Beth had intended and she braced herself for a reprimand. But the faintest of smiles momentarily deepened the wrinkles on Strange's weathered face.

"Loyalty. I like that." He glanced up at the map. "But from what you say, I think I now must, reluctantly, put soldiers into all the streets on the route—"

"No, sir. I think know how to save Polly without *any* danger to the King."

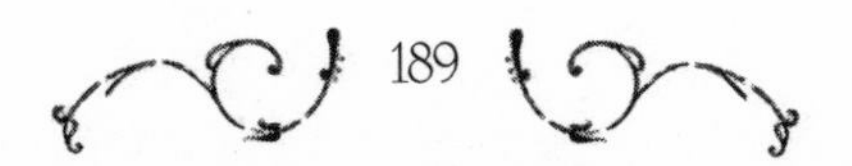

"You surely don't wish me to cancel the trip or change the route? That would only alert Vale and may well *trigger* Polly's death."

"No, no changes. Everything must go ahead as planned."

The spymaster frowned. "Beth, I have given you a great deal of latitude. Now, your team is scattered and in danger, and I have specific intelligence of the threat to His Majesty. If anything were to go wrong because one of my young spies asked for indulgence, just how long do you think my head would remain attached to my neck?"

"B-but you must hear me out, sir. You must!"

His steely grey eyes bore into her for a moment. "Then tell me of your plan."

Beth sighed in relief. "First, I need to see one of your guards…"

Chapter Eighteen

Assassination

John's legs were stiff and sore from crouching in his hiding place, but he daren't move. Groby had placed men at the other end of the alley to prevent casual passers-by from entering, and to alert them to anyone that Strange may have sent. He felt the wooden stock of the pistol against his ribs with every breath – a constant reminder of the terrible dilemma he faced. He had lost track of the time but he knew it couldn't be long before he would be required to make the terrible decision. Unless Beth arrived with Strange to save the day, he would find himself face to face with the King, pointing a pistol.

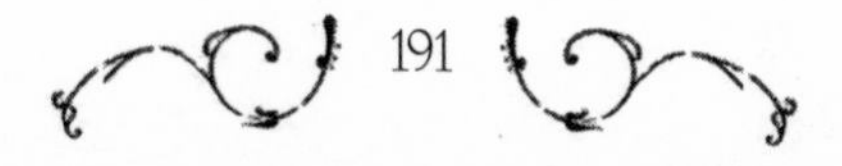

He could hardly believe that they had forced him into this position, where he might have to betray his oath to protect the King. Would he fire? *Could* he? And even if Beth and Strange did arrive, what if they hadn't traced Polly first? What if Ralph wasn't able to stop Groby's men from harming his sister? John worried he might find himself having to ignore their intervention and still kill the King to save his sister's life. His stomach twisted with the impossibility of the quandary he was in.

Then he heard a nearby church bell chiming quarter to the hour. Nine? Or the fateful hour of ten? The answer was quick in coming.

There was a sudden shuffling as Groby and Vale adjusted their positions beside him and began to ready themselves.

"Any minute now," Vale told his henchman.

John felt a strong hand come down hard on his shoulder and fix it in a vice-like grip. "The moment approaches, lad. Your sister or the King. Be ready."

John's hands felt cold and limp, despite the warm sunshine that had now broken through the clouds, and his whole body began to shake. Even if he did try to shoot the King, how true would be his aim? Should he miss deliberately? Questions kept swirling in his mind.

Then he heard distant voices – strident, urgent. Soldiers barking orders, echoing off the walls at the bottom of Woodrofe Lane. And soon after came the clip-clopping of horses' hooves on cobblestones, and the clatter of carriage wheels.

The King's carriage.

He raised his head and peered over the upturned table that was his hiding place. He could see it now: a large open carriage painted a shiny black with trimmings of gold leaf. The four horses wore colourful plumes that swayed and nodded as they moved; two drivers in royal livery sat at the front. There were three other people inside the carriage beside the King. Two wore scarlet robes lined with white ermine, while the third wore much drabber, plain clothes. He had his back to John, but just from his outline John knew it was Strange. The King himself was partly obscured by the people surrounding him, but John could see that he wore purple robes also trimmed with white fur, including a voluminous hood pulled over the flowing black locks of his trademark black wig. Four mounted soldiers rode in front of the carriage in pairs, and six behind. They carried spears aloft with purple ribbons fluttering near the tips, and wore gleaming silver body armour. Swords hung from their belts. John knew

these were the men who would fall on him and hack him to pieces the instant he discharged his gun at the King…

But where was Beth?

The horses and carriage rattled to within a few feet of the alley. To John in his terror, the sound of the hooves and wheels rumbling along the stony surface was suddenly deafening, filling his head with such noise it threatened to overwhelm him. He was suddenly paralysed, and the gun almost seemed to throb against his chest as if it was willing him to use it.

Groby's voice snapped him back into reality. "*Now, Turner! Now – or, by God, your sister's life!*"

John sprang up and ran, but it no longer felt like it was his own body surging towards the King. It was as if he floated like a ghost, like this was a dream.

The carriage continued, but heads turned, voices shouted.

"Mister Strange!" John shouted, suddenly finding his voice. "I am with Sir Alan Strange, the spymaster, and I must warn the King of a threat to his life!"

The carriage was almost past him now. Why didn't it stop?

Just when he thought his chance had gone, an order was barked and the carriage rattled to a halt. The King's

back was towards him, almost within pistol-shot.

"I am here by the order of the King's spymaster!" John repeated. It seemed to cause some confusion and hesitation among the guards, and gave him precious seconds to get closer. As he did so, he slipped his hand inside his coat and gripped the handle of the pistol. It felt heavy and alien against his sweating palm. As the King rose and began to turn to see what was happening, Strange rose too, putting himself between John and the King – but John could still see the back of the King's hooded head. He glanced back at where Groby and Vale were hiding, but knew he wouldn't be able to alert the guards without ruining any chance of seeing Polly alive again. He whipped the pistol out and aimed.

May God forgive me…

To his amazement, Strange ducked as soon as he saw the pistol, while the King continued to turn around. John tried to focus. He tightened his finger on the trigger, but his head was ready to explode – a swirl of screams and flashing lights – and he froze. He knew in that moment that nothing could ever make him betray the King. He aimed the gun away into the air, hoping desperately that in the mêlée he could alert the guards to where Groby and Vale lay in wait. Then, a guard dashed towards him

with a cry, and finally John fired.

It was as if time slowed down. He saw the flash of the gun as it jerked in his hand. He saw the cloud of black smoke emerge from it, and breathed in the acrid smell of gunpowder. He saw out of the corner of his eye the tip of a guard's spear thrusting towards him in a blur – but too late to stop him.

And through the smoke he saw the King fall.

John stood like a statue, his face white and frozen in horror, the pistol still outstretched in his hand. *How? I … I wasn't aiming for him?*

A cry from Strange woke him from the spell and suddenly time was running normally again.

"HOLD! TAKE HIM ALIVE!"

Strange had grabbed the soldier's spear but too late to stop the point slicing through John's coat. He felt a sudden pain as if a red–hot poker had been plunged into his shoulder. The other soldiers were converging now, halted at the sound of Strange's voice. Their weapons were drawn, but with John surrounded, all eyes were on the carriage in which the King lay, shot at point-blank range. One of the men in robes was bending over the fallen, unmoving body. He slowly rose, his face ashen.

"He is gone. The … the King is no more."

John felt rough hands grabbing him from all sides as panic and confusion gripped his mind. He was *sure* he had aimed away from the King … . But now he was a traitor and a murderer. Surely nothing now could save him from the gallows.

I did it for you, Polly…

John was numb, in a daze, barely aware of the journey to the Tower. He weakly allowed himself to be manhandled into a building, vaguely aware that it was not a dungeon but some sort of soldiers' barrack room.

"Leave him to me," he heard Strange say. "You have done well today, men."

Done well? What did he mean? The King was dead! Did he mean Polly? Had they found her?

"W-where's my sister? Is she found?" John said weakly. "I … I don't understand what happened … My aim … I was aiming away—"

"No talking until I show you what you have done."

Just then, the door opened and four soldiers shuffled in, carrying a body in purple robes.

John turned away. "No! I don't want to see. Take me

to the dungeons!"

"Why would they take you to the dungeons?" asked a familiar voice. A man emerged from an office at the end of the room. He wore only a white shirt and breeches, no wig; it took John a few seconds to register who it was, and even then he refused to believe it.

"Your Majesty…?"

The King laughed, and just then the figure being carried into the room began to squirm.

"Enough," Strange commanded the soldiers. "We're out of sight of prying eyes now."

"I can see why she is considered such a good actress!" said one of the soldiers.

Still in the men's arms, Beth sat up and faced John. Her purple robes slipped open, revealing a metal breastplate. She knocked on it with her knuckles, and looked at John with a smile.

"'Tis a good thing I'm so tall for a young woman, is it not?" Beth said. "We managed a decoy quite well. I was certain you wouldn't aim at me. I just knew it." She looked at Strange, and her smile widened. "Though I'm grateful for the loan of this armour…"

"Some quite admirable improvization on Miss Johnson's part still let Vale and his cohorts think you'd achieved their nefarious plot," Strange added, but then his expression darkened. "Unfortunately, the scum are still at large."

"But … I … you…" John gasped. Then the room began to swim and blur. He started to sway – and everything went black.

Chapter Nineteen

Circle of Flames

Beth put her arm round John's shoulders. He had just come round and was sitting up in one of the soldiers' beds, a mug of water in his hands. She wished she could do more for him. Having just learned of their decoy plan and its success – but that his sister remained unfound and that Groby and Vale had got away – the poor man's mind was in turmoil.

"How? How could they have got away with Strange's spies everywhere?"

Beth sighed. "I know. Vale had lots of his own men in the area who obviously helped them escape – I don't doubt he had a plan mapped out for their escape. There was a big, chaotic fight and somehow in all the confusion they slipped through the net."

John's face reddened. "This is all my fault. If only I could have thought of another way to stop them before all this happened – or taken them out somehow myself? But instead I came so close to shooting the K—"

"No." Beth interrupted, looking at him sternly. "You didn't. John, you did exactly what you had to. You were backed into a corner and yet you still acted to protect His Majesty. Fear not – Strange's spies and the King's guards are out looking for them. In all the panic caused by the fire and the streets full of people, it's going to be really difficult to find them, I fear, but you know we'll do our best. We just need to think where to start..."

"Fire?" said John vacantly. "I'd forgotten about the fire."

Beth smoothed down his ruffled hair. "I'm not surprised after all you've been through. But I'm afraid it's still raging as badly as ever. Half the city is gone, and the rest is in grave danger."

"Then wherever Polly is—"

"Wherever she is, she's with Ralph. The gang were going to take him to her, remember? I'm sure he can come up with some sort of trick to fool her guards and get her away. You know how good he is at that sort of thing. And as soon as he gets word to us, we'll find them." Beth hoped she sounded more confident than she felt. She was also worried about the consequences if Ralph made a mistake and showed he wasn't truly on the kidnappers' side, then wasn't able to get away…

"They will be watching him like hawks," John said, echoing her thoughts. He tilted his head to one side, frowning. "But there's one thing that has been bothering me…"

"All that's happened the last couple of days and there's only one thing that's bothering you?" she teased gently.

But he didn't smile. "The rhyme. Polly's answer to one of the questions."

"What – do you think they tricked you?"

"No, no. They could never have come up with that; it's not even a well-known line from the song. You would say 'Oranges and lemons' or 'Give me five farthings' or something wouldn't you? Why did she choose that line, 'Kettles and pans'?"

Beth wasn't sure where this was heading, but she felt a sudden tingle of anticipation. "What comes next? I can't remember it that well."

"Say the bells of St Ann's..."

"Is Ann a favourite name of hers? A friend?"

"Not that I know of, but I've been thinking – Blackfriars church is called St Ann's. What if ... what if that's where they've taken her? She might have been trying to tell us something?"

Beth felt her heart quicken with hope – but it soon mingled with fear. "The fire's been heading towards Blackfriars..."

"What? Oh my goodness. Polly! What if she's there and the fire's already too close, and—"

"Hold on," Beth said, reaching out a hand to calm him. "If the fire's been causing an obstruction, Groby won't have been able to have got word to his men to ... hurt her. And with any luck, our ruse worked and they think the King is really dead! Groby's men would be so afraid of failing to follow orders they would stay 'til the very last minute, waiting for word to set her free or—"

John stood up, not letting Beth finish. "If there's even a chance we're right and she's at Blackfriars, we've got to get there ourselves – with all haste!"

* * *

It felt wrong to be heading straight towards a place where it seemed the sky itself was on fire. Pressing through the crowds coming in the opposite direction, Beth and John tried to ignore the bemused looks that anyone should be in such a hurry to head towards danger. By the time they reached the Fleet River, the bridge was a frenzied bottleneck. Rather than trying to force a way against the tide of humanity, Beth veered to the right and led John down the grassy bank to the water's edge. The river was actually little more than a ditch at this point – stinking and muddy, but fordable.

"We'll get out feet wet, but 'tis the only way," she said, beginning to make her way across.

"I've a feeling they'll soon dry out," John replied grimly, looking at the fire ahead of them. "Part of me just prays to God that we're wrong, and Polly isn't at St Ann's."

"The fire's spreading unevenly. There seem to be a few gaps," Beth gasped as they scrambled up the other side, their feet squelching in their shoes.

Rather than coming back up onto the pandemonium of Ludgate Hill, Beth headed for a tiny opening further down the Fleet leading to an alley. It was so narrow it was like entering a dark tunnel, though one lined with

ancient, ramshackle houses. Even here, people were still emerging with their arms full of children and the few goods they owned. Eventually the alley opened out onto a wider street.

"I know this place," said John. "We're in Blackfriars now – St Ann's is just down the road on the right."

But when they tried to run towards Puddle Dock Hill, which led past the entrance to the church down to the Thames, a wall of flames confronted them. The heat was so intense that Beth and John jumped back and cowered round the corner. They waited, listening to the crackling house timbers, and the little explosions as glass in windows was heated beyond breaking point all along the street. Beth heard something fall near her feet and expected to see a burning splinter of wood, but it was a pigeon. Its wing feathers were blackened and scorched beyond use, and it writhed vainly on the ground. Before she could do anything, it stopped moving, its eyes staring sightlessly towards the fire that had ended its life.

"There must be another way!" cried John, bringing her back to reality. He ran ahead to another, even narrower alleyway, which took them deeper into the labyrinth of back streets. It brought them to Ireland Yard, a rat-infested, rubbish-strewn thoroughfare – but at the end

of it Beth could see a church. It was framed by leaping red flames, but the building itself was untouched.

"That's got to be it! There's still time!"

They sprinted down Ireland Yard, stopping at the point where it opened out onto the little churchyard of St Ann's. The shadows of the gravestones danced eerily in the light of the fire raging in the background.

"Coast looks clear," John whispered.

Just as he spoke, one of the big stained-glass windows shattered and pieces of glass in reds, blues and greens tinkled across the paving stones that encircled the church. They both jumped, but after a moment Beth edged closer.

"At least now we can look inside before we try to get in," she said in a low voice. She crossed the churchyard in a crouching run, then pressed herself flat against the stone wall of the church itself. They felt like fire bricks, almost too hot to touch. John joined her, and slowly raised his head an inch at a time 'til his eyes were above the jagged row of coloured glass left in the bottom of the frame. He quickly ducked back down, stifling a little cry. His chest was heaving rapidly.

"Are they in there?" Beth hissed. "Have you been spotted?"

John couldn't bring himself to speak. Beth cautiously raised her own head up to take a look.

There was a group of people in front of the altar. One was a burly, dark-haired man, another was Ed Hewer, who stood beside Ralph himself – and all three formed a circle round Polly. She was tied to a chair, a dirty gag covering her mouth leaving just her wide, terrified eyes visible. On her lap was her much-loved doll, Lucinda.

"I don't care what Groby said," the dark-haired man was saying. "If we don't get out now we'll all be burned alive, and then it won't *matter* how much he's paying us."

"The girl must be dealt with," Hewer insisted. "We've had no word from Groby, which means something must have gone wrong. If she isn't taken care of, I'm a dead man myself. Besides, the job's worth a *lot* of money to me."

"Oh? And how much might that be? More than we're gettin', I'll wager."

"That's between me and Groby. I work for him, not you."

"But I'm sure he'd be interested to know you've hired someone *else* to do your dirty work – an outsider we know nothing about."

"Ed knows me well enough," Ralph said flatly. "I've

been in enough trouble in the past. If I get caught again for so much as stealin' an apple it'll be the noose for me, so I'm hardly likely to blab, am I?"

The man who had been speaking took a step towards Ralph, and as he did so he pulled out a knife.

"That makes sense – assuming you're tellin' the truth…" He pressed the tip to Ralph's throat, drawing a small dot of blood. Beth was impressed by the way her friend didn't flinch. Even when everyone's attention was drawn to more windows cracking, he remained impassive, his eyes on the man with the deadly weapon. Finally the man then turned the knife round so that the handle was facing Ralph.

"Here, then. Do it. Let's not waste any more time."

John joined Beth at the window, swallowing hard. "Oh, Lord…"

Ralph was adjusting the knife in his hand, getting a feel for its weight and balance. He turned towards Polly.

"He won't do it, John, of course he won't."

"How can he get out of it?"

"This is Ralph we're talking about. He'll think of something."

Still, she watched closely, her heart beating fast as Ralph slowly advanced on the petrified girl until he

was looming over her. He snaked the point of the blade towards her throat just as the man had done to him…

Beth could see Ralph mouth something to Polly, and she nodded almost imperceptibly, but before Ralph had to do anything more, the tension was broken by a resounding *CRACK*. It was the sound of crashing timber coming from somewhere inside the tower of the church.

All eyes turned upwards. The ceiling remained intact, but Beth noticed a spreading black patch in the cracking, sagging plaster. It was a rapidly spreading scorch mark – the spire of St Ann's was on fire. Within seconds, the ceiling began to break up and crumble, showering those inside with burning debris and splinters of wood.

"*NOW!*" Beth yelled. She threw herself over the window ledge, ignoring the shards of broken glass scraping her hands and legs. John flew over so fast that he overtook her, vaulting over pews towards Ralph and his sister. Beth went for the dark-haired man, who was feverishly brushing red-hot plaster from his smoking hair and shoulders, while Hewer himself stood and looked on in helpless horror, clearly completely out of his depth.

The burly man quickly produced another knife, and Beth made a grab for it, but he was so strong that she failed to yank it from his grasp and now he turned on her.

They wrestled desperately, Beth focusing all her might on the wrist that held the knife, but the man was much too bulky and powerful. It was a battle she was doomed to lose, and she only knew she couldn't afford to let go. His stinking breath was in her face and his glinting dark eyes bore into her as they fought for possession of the weapon. With his free hand he forced her back against a pew with such force that it seemed her spine would break. She screamed in agony, but still kept her grip on his wrist. Larger pieces of burning timber were falling all around them now, and the pews themselves were catching fire. A burning beam as big as Beth herself came spinning down and fell next to her leg, the flames licking around the bottom of her skirt.

In desperation, she hooked her foot beneath it and pushed it against the man's body. She could feel smoke start to rise from her skirts – but she could also see flames erupting from the hem of her opponent's doublet. It was a battle of wills, both their hands on the knife, the heat from the burning wood becoming unbearable against Beth's leg, the man's eyes darting from hers to his burning clothing. With one last effort, he pushed against her with all his might. She toppled over the back of the pew into the row behind, losing her grip on the knife. With a look of malevolent glee he leaned over the pew and raised the weapon over her. Beth was in a heap, helpless to defend herself.

But then, without warning, the kidnapper was no longer visible.

There was a *whoosh*, and all Beth could see was a pillar of fire. His doublet was ablaze, the knife was forgotten and he was screaming and manically patting at the flames that engulfed him. As Beth picked herself up, the man tore off his tunic and threw it away, some of his other clothing still alight as he ran through a door leading to the crypt beneath the church, slamming the door shut behind him. She whirled around, still ready to fight, but she saw Hewer now trapped under another fallen beam, struggling to free himself.

Looking across the church between the other fallen, burning timbers, she saw Ralph slicing through Polly's ropes with the knife he'd been given. He and John then gathered her and her doll up and carried her, feet still bound, towards the door. Beth went to join them, but to her horror she saw that the door too was blocked by fallen debris.

"The window!" Beth cried, the heat against her face almost unbearable now, and every breath searing her

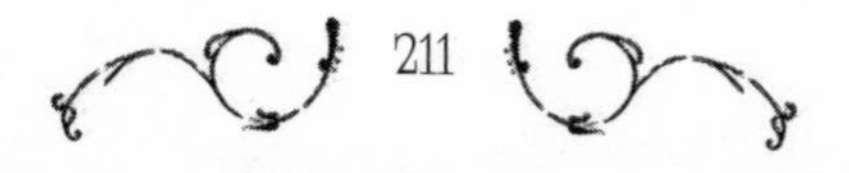

lungs. She led them to the broken window where they'd entered, kicking at pieces of fiery timber to clear their path as she went. She scrambled out first, then took Polly as Ralph and John passed her over. Just when it seemed they were getting away, she saw Polly pointing at something over her shoulder.

"Look out!"

Beth twisted round and saw that the long grass in the churchyard, dry and yellow from the summer drought, was also on fire now, and the wind was pushing it rapidly in their direction. Soon, the church would be at the centre of a circle of flames.

Beth spotted a big, elaborate tombstone for some wealthy parishioner leaning up against the back wall of the churchyard. Getting the little girl to cling onto her back, Beth shouted to the others to follow her. They all managed to scramble on top of the monument just before the flames reached them.

Ralph and John helped Polly over the wall and into the street on the other side, and while she waited Beth allowed herself a final look back. Behind a curtain of flames, she saw Hewer through the window of the church, clearly still trapped. Their eyes met for an instant, then there was a crackling and a rumbling, rapidly increasing

in intensity. The upper part of the wall on that side of the church fell in, bringing half the roof down with it in a cloud of smoke and dust, and Hewer could be seen no more.

"Come on, Beth!" John shouted from the top of the wall, holding his hand out to her. We'll be trapped if we don't run *now*!"

With his help, she clambered out of the churchyard. The fire had reached the end of Ireland Yard now, with long flames leaping out of a butcher's shop on the corner, almost closing that route off. Ralph, who was in the lead, hesitated when he saw the red and orange tongues of flame licking hungrily across their path. But John ran straight past him, carrying Polly on his back now, and covering her face with his free hand. "Keep running as fast as you can – there's no other way out!"

Ralph put a spurt on and followed them through the flames, with Beth close behind. She felt the heat scorching her skin and smelled her hair singeing, but it took only a second to come out on the other side. Ralph's coat sleeve was on fire, and Beth helped him quickly to pat it out.

But the danger still wasn't over.

Fleet Street was ablaze beyond the bridge now, and

every way they tried to take was blocked by the fire. It soon became clear that while they'd been in the church the fire had overtaken them, at least on the northern side of the city. But by following the fleeing inhabitants, they found themselves on the last open route down to the river. People were pouring through the legal district where the Inns of Court were situated. Beth was being almost carried along, half off her feet, by the densely packed throng down to the Thames, and then along its banks towards Temple Stairs. There, boats of all shapes and sizes were ferrying escapees further west or across to Southwark on the other side, where she could see crowds lining the river bank. They were looking on in awed silence like spectators at a ghastly play.

Beth and the others could see that from here it would easy to move further west along the shore if the fire should pursue them. They decided to rest for a moment, and sat on a decaying, upturned rowing boat at the water's edge, panting hard. Only now did Beth truly realize how absolutely shattered, grimy and hungry she was. Her remaining energy seemed to drain away all at once now that the danger had passed, and she slumped forwards. After other adventures she'd had to come up with an excuse for her scars and torn clothing, but for

once everyone in London looked the same or worse. No one would ever guess what she and her companions had been through.

Ralph had flopped onto his back, and John was next to him, gazing down at the exhausted Polly who had curled up in a ball with her doll. He looked amazed to finally have his sister back, and rubbed her shoulder soothingly.

"We did it," Beth murmured.

John's brown eyes, weary but shining with the light of relief and triumph out of a soot-smeared face, held hers for a moment. "Thank you, Beth. I'd never have got Polly back without you."

She took out her handkerchief and wiped away a black stain from the tip of his nose, and he caught her hand before she could take it away. They were interrupted by a loud cough.

"Yes – thanks Beth," said Ralph. "He would never have done it without *you*. If only you'd had more help. A third person, with a nautical background perhaps … ?"

"Oh, Ralph!" John exclaimed in dismay. "Of course I couldn't have done it without you either! I didn't mean…"

Ralph burst out laughing and sat up, slapping John

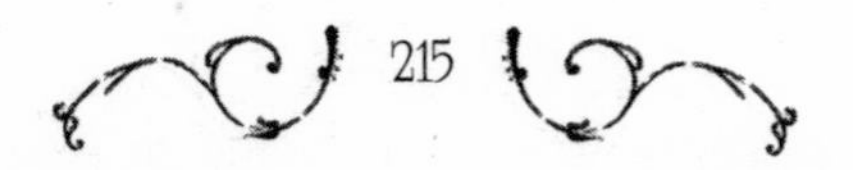

so hard on the back he almost fell off the upturned boat. "Just kiddin', matey! We're a team – but some might think Beth's a bit prettier than me. I don't want *you* gazing into my eyes and wiping my nose, so no hard feelings."

"But Beth just … I mean, I…"

Ralph laughed again and John stopped talking, blushing hard even through the dirt on his face.

"Come on," Beth said, suddenly feeling more energetic. "Enough sitting around. Anyone would think we've just saved the life of the King and young Polly here in one day!" She stood up. "Let's get out of here."

Chapter Twenty

Aftermath

Ralph knew London like the back of his hand – every wide thoroughfare, every little back alley and dingy yard. And yet, picking his way through the ruined, smouldering streets he knew so well, he finally admitted to himself that he was lost.

It was disorienting, even frightening, like a dream from which he couldn't wake himself. Here he was right in the centre of his home town, gazing about like the country bumpkins on their first visit to the capital who he used to snigger at, lost and bewildered. Supposedly he was not far from where the Mercer's Hall used to

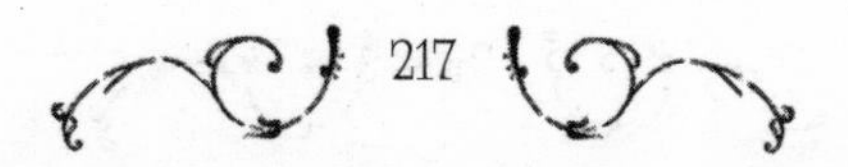

stand. Huge lumps of grey, blackened metal lay among the charred timbers and bricks of ruined buildings. Was this the remains of the lead roof of the Hall, or was he in another district altogether?

Nothing looked the same. Landmarks that had been there for ever had been destroyed in three days. He could only head towards the afternoon sun as it sank in the west, shimmering orange behind the heat haze and thin pall of smoke still issuing from the ruins of a great city. With every step he scrunched through cinders and smoking rubble, through pieces of bizarrely twisted glass from the many shattered windows. His feet were beginning to burn as the heat leached through the soles of his thin, cheap boots.

He came across an old man, bent and careworn, sifting through the wreckage of what must once had been his home. A woman of a similar age sat on all that was left of the staircase: three splintered, charred steps leading to nowhere. Her head was bowed, and she was clutching a portrait in a blackened frame, quietly weeping to herself.

Ralph had arranged to meet John at the Old Bailey, only to finally navigate through the devastation and find that the famous courthouse wasn't there any more. Luckily, John was.

"'When will you pay me?' say the bells of Old Bailey…" he muttered under his breath as they both surveyed what had once been the courthouse. "I still can't believe it."

"At least it stopped short of wiping out the whole of London," Ralph replied.

"What about Culpeper?"

"He's fine. I found out he went to stay with his brother in Islington 'til it was safe to come back. Is Polly all right?"

"Yes. She's having nightmares and she's still a bit nervous about going outside, but the children in the street will look after her when I'm not around. And she knows the 'bad men' have gone and won't be coming back."

"Can we be sure about that, though? Vale and Groby seem like cats with nine lives," Ralph said as they walked together through the rubble.

"But they must have used up at least half of them by now. Besides, if they make another attempt on the King, I doubt they would use the same tactics again."

Rumours about an attempt on the King's life had spread in the days following the crisis near the Navy Board, but the King had already emerged to prove to the

public he was unharmed. He'd let it be known that some brave, loyal subjects had once again foiled a secret plot against him…

As they headed further west, they began to encounter houses and churches unaffected by the inferno. Eventually they reached a district where, with their backs to the desolation, it was possible to believe there had never been a raging fire at all. And finally they arrived at their destination: the King's Theatre, Drury Lane.

"Look!" said John.

They both grinned. Adorning the walls were posters proclaiming the very first performance of the Company's latest play:

The Most Excellent & Lamentable Tragedie

of

THE EMPIRE DIES

Mr Samuel Jones..............Alaric

Mr Benjamin Lovett..............Emperor Honorius

Mistress Beth Johnson..............Flavia

"*But what sayest you, fair Flavia? Triumphant I may be, but I have slain so many of your fellow Romans. How can you still love such a monster as me?*"

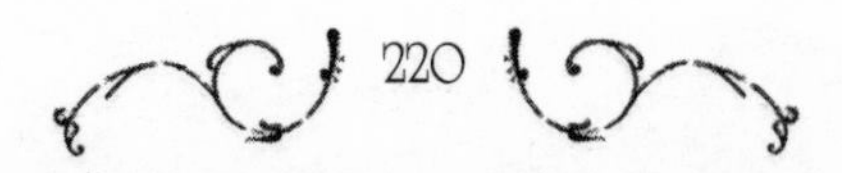

Beth and Samuel Jones were sitting among the ruins of Rome – or at least the King's Theatre version of it. Samuel had proved to be a marvellous actor and had helped her enormously, but Beth was just about to utter her last line in the play and she dreaded the reaction she might get. In comedies, the laughter told her how well things were going, and if necessary she could make changes during the performance. The only way to tell a tragedy hadn't gone down well was when people began booing and throwing rotten fruit at the end rather than applauding. There had been total silence for this whole last scene – did it mean they were captivated or bored?

"I prithee hear me, Alaric, when I say that empires may rise and fall but mine love for thee shall *never* die!"

As Beth moved to the front of the stage, she curtseying and Samuel bowing, the audience rose like a rippling, inrushing wave; applause and cries of approval echoed around the auditorium. In one of the front rows, Beth caught a glimpse of a beaming John and Ralph leading the ovation. Ralph stuck his fingers into his mouth and let out a whistle so piercing it even cut through the thunderous acclaim.

She turned to pick out Maisie among the extras at the back of the stage, her face aglow – her friend was

resplendent in her Roman noblewoman's costume, and she looked as if she had been on stage all her life. Half of London came to see these plays, and it crossed Beth's mind that perhaps Maisie's father could be here, little realizing he was enjoying his own daughter's performance. Out of the corner of her eye she also spotted a grinning William Huntingdon in the wings, applauding with gusto. Beth felt a warm glow inside, and the hint of a tear in her eye. She was no longer just a comedienne. She'd been a success in her tasks both as a spy and now as an actress. Things could only get better from here.

Epilogue

A group of men sifted through the still-smoking wreckage of what once had been St Ann's, Blackfriars. One pulled aside bits of fallen masonry and fished out a silver candlestick holder, twisted and bent by the intense heat 'til it resembled a bizarre, strangled, swan's neck. The clergyman, in his black coat and broad white collar, plucked out a singed but surprisingly intact Bible from under the remains of the lectern. The early September sun shone down on them, but the mood was sombre. Buildings like this had stood for centuries, and even though they might be replaced, things would never be

the same again. Faint echoes of countless generations of worshippers: silent prayers, joyful christenings, mournful funerals, lingered within the very stones of places like St Ann's. Like the fragrance of a flower trampled underfoot, those memories were gone for ever.

The silence was broken by a shout, and a man's head emerged from below. It was as if a soul from one of the graves beneath the aisle had been disturbed by the destruction of his eternal resting place. But he was one of the searchers.

"A body!" he cried. "In the crypt. Too bad to recognize..."

But as he watched from inside a burnt-out, half-collapsed house in Ireland Yard, one man nearby knew who the perished man was without needing to see him. His own men had already checked through the ruins of the church. They'd managed to pull out one poor soul from the wreckage, barely breathing and badly burned, before the authorities arrived. Sir Henry Vale had considered neatening the situation by leaving the wretched man to expire amongst the smouldering beams, but thought better of it. Saving a man's life buys a special kind of loyalty.

Before the officials brought the remaining body out

of the church, Vale turned his back on the scene and walked away.

But he would never forget this day.

Everyone, from that coxcomb of a King to those who worked in the shadows to keep him on his false throne, would pay for preventing Sir Henry Vale's plans.

He shook his head. "Time for a longer game, I think…" he muttered to himself as he walked away.

Cast of Characters

BETH JOHNSON

Actress extraordinaire at the King's Theatre and – unbeknownst to her admiring audience – a much-valued spy. Tall and beautiful with chestnut brown hair and green eyes, Beth has risen from lowly depths as a foundling abandoned on the steps of Bow Church to become a celebrated thespian and talented espionage agent.

SIR ALAN STRANGE

Tall, dark and mysterious, spymaster Alan Strange seeks out candidates from all walks of life, spotting the potential for high-quality agents in the most unlikely of places. Ruthless but fair, Strange is an inspiration for his recruits, and trains them well.

RALPH CHANDLER

Former street urchin Ralph has lead a rough-and-tumble existence, but his nefarious beginnings have their uses when employed in his role as one of Sir Alan Strange's spies, working in the service of the King.

JOHN TURNER

Junior clerk at the Navy Board, handsome John imagines himself in more daring, adventurous circumstances – and he soon has the opportunity when he meets Beth Johnson and becomes part of her gang of spies.

SIR HENRY VALE

Criminal mastermind and anti-King conspirator, Sir Henry Vale was supposedly executed by beheading in 1662 for his attempt to take the King's life – but all may not be as it seems…

EDMUND GROBY

Squat, swarthy and with one ominous finger missing from his left hand, Groby is a relentless villain and loyal henchman. He hates the monarchy and all it represents, and will stop at nothing to prevent our gang from derailing the King-killer's plans.

MAISIE WHITE

A young orange-seller at the theatre where Beth works, Maisie has been quickly taken under the older girl's wing – but she knows nothing of her friend's double life as a spy…

Dear Reader,

I hope you have enjoyed this book. While Beth Johnson and her friends are fictitious characters, the world that they inhabit is based on history.

During Beth's time, fires were a frequent occurrence amongst the crowded streets of London. Houses were built from wood, and were packed closely together. If one house was set alight, the flames could quickly carry across to neighbouring buildings.

On 2nd September 1666, after a hot, dry summer, a fire started in a bakery on Pudding Lane. It quickly spread across a huge area of London, wreaking havoc. There was no fire brigade ready with fire engines and pressure hoses to douse the flames with water like there is today. People had to make do with bailing water by hand and tearing down buildings to stop the blaze from spreading further. More than 13,000 houses were destroyed in the fire, leaving around one sixth of London's population homeless. Lasting five days, it was the worst fire in the history of London.

Jo Macauley

Read on for a sneak peek of the next
Secrets & Spies adventure, New World…

New World

The ship's name was *Dreadnought*, but that name no longer suited her. To look at the state she was in as she lay moored in Portsmouth Harbour, you would think the tattered hulk would have a good deal to dread. The ship's carpenter had done the best he could to patch her up, but his repairs looked like make-up on a week-old corpse. If the wind blew too sudden and strong, the mainmast would topple like a rotten old oak. The boards were split below the waterline, and tarred rags could only keep the sea out for so long.

Her captain, Hugh Tucker, didn't look too healthy

himself. In a dockside inn not far from where his ship was berthed, he sat across the table from a fat man in a wig. Candlelight lit Tucker's face from below, turning it into a gaunt, bearded skull.

"I don't like this job, and I don't like you," Tucker said. He was on to his third cup of wine, and it had freed his tongue from politeness.

"You aren't being paid to like either," the fat man said. "My employer is paying you to take his ship where he wants it to go, carrying the cargo he chooses to export."

"Cargo!" Tucker shook his head in disgust.

The fat man shrugged. "A commodity like any other."

"You call a hold full of prisoners a commodity?"

"Don't tell me you've developed a conscience." Lucius Bebbington, the fat man, sounded bitter and bored. He took a large fingerful of snuff. "It doesn't suit you, Captain Tucker. Not with your reputation."

"It's not that!" Tucker grimaced. "And it's not the money, either. The money's good enough. But your employer wants me to pack 'em in like so much stovewood!"

"The *Dreadnought* is a large ship," Bebbington pointed out.

"But three hundred? It'd be like piloting Newgate

Prison across the blasted Atlantic."

"The more prisoners we can ship to America, the more the government will pay. It's sound economic sense."

"And if we never reach America?" Tucker said, glowering over the candle. "What then? Look, you've seen the state of the *Dreadnought*. That storm off Penzance practically crippled her."

"She's seaworthy enough."

"If your mysterious employer would just fork out for repairs…"

"Oh, let's not open this casket of worms again." Bebbington rolled his eyes. "If you'd kept to the agreed course, you'd never have run into that storm in the first place."

"I told you, the Dutch would have been on us if I hadn't!"

"My dear Captain, calm down. Do you want everyone to know our business?"

Tucker filled a pipe with shaking hands. Bebbington watched impassively while he lit it.

"It ain't like we'd be transporting cattle nor coal," Tucker protested. "These are criminals. They outnumber the crew! What if there's an escape, a mutiny?"

"It's your job to make sure there isn't one."

"And you're overloading a damaged ship! The weight of that many people … if we run into another storm…"

Bebbington leaned over the table. "Don't quote me, but I'm sure my employer won't mind if you throw one or two overboard," he whispered. "Lightens the load *and* serves as a warning to the others. Two birds with one stone, eh?"

Captain Tucker looked sick.

Bebbington stood up abruptly. "You have your orders," he said. "The *Dreadnought* will sail on the fourteenth, as agreed. Oh, cheer up, damn you! This time next year, you will be a rich man."

Tucker swept his hat on to his head. "Your obedient servant, sir," he said. He stumbled out of the inn without a backward glance.

The night was cold and a sea mist had drifted in. It quickly leeched away what little warmth the wine he'd drunk had provided. Tucker pulled his coat around him and cursed the weather, the sea, that fat pig Bebbington and his blasted employer most of all.

Up ahead, the looming shape of the *Dreadnought* made Tucker shiver even more. He thought of three hundred convicts, crammed into that fragile wooden hull. Desperate sorts, all of them. Thieves. Beggars.

Scum, with nothing to lose.

Suddenly he was very afraid.

"Damned souls," he whispered hoarsely to himself. "And me, the captain of the ship chartered to take them down to Hell."

Meanwhile, back at the inn, Bebbington was welcoming a colleague to his table.

"You talked him round, then?" the man asked. "I thought he was going to swing for you for a moment."

"Men of the sea are like dogs," Bebbington said, with a tight smile. "They're not happy unless you keep them in their place. Whip 'em once in a while. Show 'em who's boss."

"He'll sail?"

"He must. And he knows it."

"Then here's to prosperity," the man said, raising his glass. "Gold uncounted. Riches galore."

"A fair wind, a calm sea, and hundreds of golden guineas in the bank," Bebbington agreed.

They clinked glasses and drank.

Bebbington smacked his lips. "I can't wait to tell Mister Vale the good news. He'll be so pleased with the two of us!"

Read New World and continue the adventure!

Look out for more
Secrets & Spies adventures…

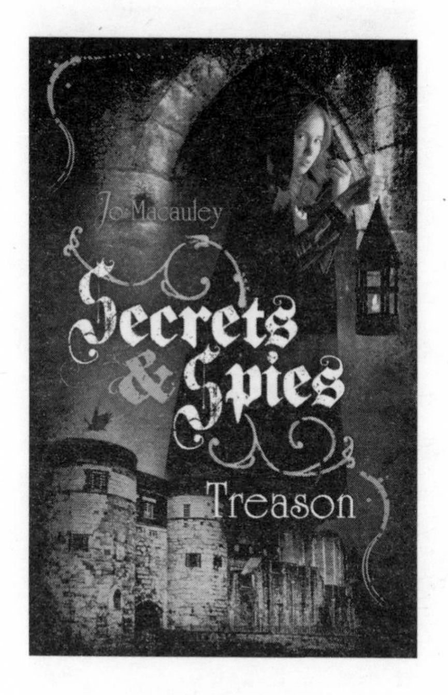

Treason

The year is 1664, and somebody wants the King dead. One November morning, a mysterious ghost ship drifts up the Thames. Sent to investigate, fourteen-year-old Beth quickly finds herself embroiled in a dangerous adventure that takes her right into the Tower of London. Will Beth be able to unravel the plot to kill the King before it's too late?

Plague

A terrible plague is sweeping through London, and Beth and her company of actors are sent to Oxford to entertain the King's court, which has decamped to avoid the deadly disease. However, Beth soon finds herself recalled to London by spymaster Alan Strange, and together with her friends and fellow spies, she must uncover a conspiracy that is taking advantage of the turmoil in the capital. A conspiracy that leads right to the seat of power…

New World

When it seems Henry Vale is planning to extend his conspiracy to kill the King to an elaborate plot in the Americas, Beth is offered the role of a lifetime. Strange, her spymaster, requests that Beth and her fellow spies travel to the new world to maintain their close surveillance of the would-be king-killer. But will their passage across the ocean be interrupted before it even begins?